**"SHALL WE GO, MRS. KINKIRK?"
KEVIN ASKED LUCY.
"CERTAINLY, MR. KINKIRK,"
LUCY REPLIED WITH A GIGGLE.**

With that, Lucy's new husband took her arm and led her through the room. Lucy and Kevin descended the stairs to the Glenoak Community Church special events space, a large room in the basement.

At the bottom of the stairs, Lucy distinctly heard the sound of tinkling water.

Ruthie rushed up to Lucy and Kevin. "You don't want to go in there."

Suddenly water gushed out of the room and into the hallway.

"You're flooded, Reverend," said Bill Carter, emerging from the events space in his best suit, now soaked through. "You should be emptied out in a few hours. Have to cancel the reception, though. . . ."

# 7th Heaven

## WEDDING MEMORIES

by Amanda Christie

Based on the hit TV series
created by Brenda Hampton

And based on the episode
"We Do" written by
Brenda Hampton

Random House 🏠 New York

Published in the United States by
Random House Children's Books,
a division of Random House, Inc., New York,
and simultaneously in Canada by
Random House of Canada Limited, Toronto.

www.randomhouse.com/teens

Library of Congress Control Number: 2003114462
ISBN: 0-375-82754-4

Printed in the United States of America
First Edition
10 9 8 7 6 5 4 3 2 1

RANDOM HOUSE and colophon are registered
trademarks of Random House, Inc.

# 7th Heaven

## WEDDING MEMORIES

# ONE

"Kevin! I'm home . . . and I've got them!"

Lucy Kinkirk, formerly Lucy Camden, raced up the stairs two at a time. She could hardly wait to see her husband's face. Calling his name again, she burst into the renovated apartment above the Camdens' garage, fully expecting to find Kevin waiting for her with a big grin and open arms.

When he failed to greet her at the door, Lucy suspected that her overworked husband had fallen asleep on the sofa, his long legs draped over the edge. He often dozed there, exhausted after double shifts as a patrol officer of the Glenoak Police Department.

*Either that,* thought Lucy, *or he's in the kitchen raiding the refrigerator and can't hear me calling him.*

But to Lucy's disappointment, Kevin wasn't dozing on the sofa or looting the fridge. Nor was he in the bathroom. Kevin wasn't home at all—the apartment they'd shared since their marriage a few short months ago was stone-cold empty.

Lucy dropped onto the sofa like a deflated balloon, the bundle she carried still clutched close. "How can Kevin not be here?" she grumbled to the empty room. "How . . . How inconsiderate!" He knew tonight was special, and she'd expected him to be here!

Despite her frustration, Lucy had to admit that she wasn't totally surprised by Kevin's absence. In the last few months, with two officers on the Glenoak police force on leave and a third on permanent disability, he'd been working double shifts at least three days a week.

Lucy appreciated that Kevin worked hard, and she was proud of her husband. But once in a while, Lucy wished Kevin pumped gas or made gourmet coffee— anything but police work.

That very morning, Lucy had reminded her husband that after her classes were over at the university, she was going to pick up their wedding pictures from Mr. Fuller. She remembered Kevin's words exactly. . . .

"That's great! I can't wait to see them."

Kevin had been getting ready for work. He pinned his badge to his pressed blue uniform and added, "It took so long to get them back that I was beginning to suspect Mr. Fuller had sold our photos to a tabloid."

"Very funny," Lucy replied, not the least bit amused.

To Lucy, the missing Camden-Kinkirk wedding photos were not a laughing matter. Sam Fuller, a parishioner at Reverend Camden's church, was a professional photojournalist. He had offered to photograph Lucy and Kevin's wedding and the reception that followed as a wedding present to the couple. But while Lucy and Kevin were away on their honeymoon, Mr. Fuller was suddenly sent by his newspaper to cover a breaking international story.

Weeks and weeks passed while Lucy and Kevin waited patiently to get their wedding photographs. Lucy was beginning to give up hope of *ever* seeing them.

Finally, just last week, Mr. Fuller had returned to Glenoak. With apologies for the delay, he phoned Lucy to say her photos were ready and she could pick them up today.

"No kidding," Kevin teased. "The man does work for a newspaper. He could have made a few bucks with our photos. I can see the tabloid headline now: LUCY CAMDEN WEDS! HUNDREDS OF ELIGIBLE BACHELORS DEPRESSED."

"Hundreds?"

"Okay, I underestimated you. Thousands." Kevin's killer grin flashed at his wife. "You always were a man-eater."

Hands on hips, Lucy glared fiercely at her husband. "Who told you I was a man-eater?" she demanded.

"Ruthie. And I believe her, too. Your little sister is wise in the ways of the world, and she's known you longer than I have."

Kevin grabbed Lucy and tickled her. She playfully slapped his hand away, then punched his arm.

"Hey!" Kevin cried. "Maybe Mr. Fuller sold sets of our wedding pictures to all those pathetic losers you used to date."

"They weren't losers," Lucy protested. "I dated nice guys."

"Yeah, but you didn't marry any of them. And with a set of our wedding photos, all those poor slobs could pretend they're as lucky as I am."

Lucy raised her hand to punch him again, even as she smiled at his words.

"I wouldn't do that," Kevin warned, finger raised. Then he pointed the same finger at his chest. "The badge is on. And it's a crime to assault a police officer."

Lucy lowered her fist as Kevin pulled her close for a goodbye kiss.

"Promise me you'll be here when I get home so we can look at the pictures together," Lucy pleaded.

"I'll do my best," he told her. "But if there's a police emergency or if we're shorthanded, I'll probably have to stay late no matter what I *want* to do."

"That police emergency had better be the end of the world, buster!" Lucy replied.

"I'll alert the authorities as to Mrs. Kinkirk's wishes in the matter."

Lucy raised her eyebrow. "You are the authorities, and you've been alerted—officially."

With a hug and final peck on the cheek, Lucy had sent her husband off to work. But now, despite the promise she'd tried to squeeze out of him, Kevin wasn't home, and Lucy was sitting in an empty apartment, wondering why her new husband wasn't here to share this special evening with her.

Suddenly Lucy spied a note clipped to the refrigerator with a magnet. Maybe it was from Kevin!

She rose and quickly crossed the room to read it:

*Lucy,*
 *Kevin called and told me he would be late. He said to tell you that he's very sorry and that he would make it up to you. The good news is that we're all dying to see the wedding pictures. Why don't you come down? We'll all look at them together.*

      *—Mom*

With a devastated sigh, Lucy turned and left her lonely apartment. Her cherished wedding photos were clutched tightly to her chest, and the disappointing note was crumpled tightly in her fist.

# TWO

"Oh, Mom," Lucy whispered, her wet cheek pressed against her mother's shoulder. "Is this how you feel when Dad breaks a promise to you . . . when he lets you down?"

Annie Camden winced at Lucy's harsh opinion of Kevin's actions.

"Lucy! Kevin did not let you down," Mrs. Camden insisted. "An emergency came up. He had to work late. It's nobody's fault. And I'm sure Kevin feels terrible about it."

"But tonight of all nights? He could have made an extra effort. He could have been here for me if he'd really, really tried."

"Lucy, it's out of Kevin's hands. He's a policeman. That means it's his job to take care of emergencies. He's like a doctor or a reverend like your father. You wouldn't want a doctor to stop in the middle of an operation because it was quitting time, would you?"

Lucy wiped her eyes. "I guess not."

"Kevin wanted to be home," Mrs. Camden said. "But sometimes life gets in the way of what we want. Tonight that happened to Kevin . . . and to you."

Lucy nodded, then frowned.

"It's so hard sometimes," she said. "Kevin's job is so intense . . . and my courses take up so much of my life. It just feels like Kevin and I never spend time together. And even when we do spend time in the same room, it's me doing my homework and Kevin dozing on the couch in front of the television because he's so tired from working double shifts."

"It's usually tough for newlyweds," Mrs. Camden said.

"But we've only been married a few months," said Lucy, "and already the romance seems to be gone."

"The romance will never be gone if you truly love each other," Mrs. Camden declared. "This is just a difficult time. You have to weather it, just like you weathered the storm that almost ruined your wedding. . . . It's best to always remember that hard times are part of life and part of a marriage." Mrs. Camden hugged her daughter. "That's why you pledge yourselves to each other for better *and* for worse."

Lucy dried her eyes. Then she forced herself to smile. "You're right, Mom."

Mrs. Camden grinned. "Of course I'm right."

Lucy puffed out her chest. "If Kevin can't come home tonight, then we'll just look at the wedding pictures tomorrow!"

"That's the spirit," said Mrs. Camden. "And after all the trouble you went through just to have a wedding, isn't it silly to complain about how rough life is treating you now?"

"I'll say!" Lucy cried. "We almost didn't have a wedding."

Lucy giggled at the memory. So did Mrs. Camden. Soon they were both laughing loudly.

"What's so funny?" asked Ruthie as she entered the kitchen.

"Good! I'm glad you're here, Ruthie," Mrs. Camden said. "You're just in time to see Lucy's reaction when I give her the present."

Grinning expectantly, Ruthie grabbed a chair at the kitchen table.

Lucy turned to find her mother holding a beautifully wrapped white package with a pink silk ribbon.

"Mom . . . I . . ."

"Open it," Mrs. Camden insisted. "Ruthie and I have been waiting weeks to give this to you."

"Wow!" Lucy exclaimed, taking the package. "It's so heavy."

At the kitchen table, Lucy untied the silk ribbon and tore away the wrapping paper to find a plain white box inside. Lifting the lid, Lucy gasped when she found a large silk-covered, lace-embroidered photo album with the words WEDDING MEMORIES adorning the front cover.

Underneath the title, a heart was embroidered with the names Kevin Kinkirk and Lucy Camden-Kinkirk, along with the date of their wedding ceremony.

"It's beautiful!" Lucy was so touched, she felt her eyes beginning to tear up again.

"Ruthie and I worked on it for weeks," Mrs. Camden said proudly. "And Ruthie really became an expert at embroidery, too."

"Nothing to it," Ruthie said, wiggling her fingers. "Tiny hands make close work easy. Or at least that's what Mom claimed to get some free labor out of me."

"Hey, do I look stupid?" teased Mrs. Camden. "Lucy, you may have a daughter someday. Are you taking notes?"

But Lucy was still focused on the album. "It's really so beautiful!"

"We knew you were picking up your wedding pictures today," said Mrs. Camden. "And we wanted to give you something to hold them. So we're glad you're here, even though the evening didn't work out the way you wanted it to."

Lucy rose and hugged them both.

"Tonight couldn't be better," Lucy replied. "Even if Kevin were here."

"Now," Mrs. Camden announced. "We have fresh cookies, and I'll make some hot chocolate. Then we can go into the living room and work on the album together.

That way when Kevin comes home, he'll be able to see your wedding photos beautifully arranged in your new album."

"Thanks, Mom," said Lucy. "For everything."

In no time, the three of them were settled in the Camdens' living room. The wedding album sat open on the coffee table, ready for the first photos to be inserted.

"What's going on?" Simon asked, wandering in.

"Lucy just got her wedding pictures," said Ruthie.

"Great!" said Simon, grabbing a cookie from the tray. He joined them in the circle, took a bite of his cookie, then pushed the dirty blond hair away from his face. "So, what are you waiting for?" he said. "Let's see those pictures!"

Lucy opened her bundle and drew out a thick envelope. It was heavy with photos.

"Here goes," she said, drawing out the first print.

"What a day that was!" Simon cried when he saw the photo. The picture was taken outside the Glenoak Community

Church on the night before the wedding. Through the pouring rain, Simon could barely see the Camdens arriving for the rehearsal.

"Wow, I forgot how much it rained," said Simon.

"Yeah," said Ruthie. "Water, water everywhere for three days straight. Another few days of that and Dad would have had us gathering all the animals two by two!"

"Not funny, Ruthie," said Lucy. "Not funny at all."

"But you have to admit the weather was an issue," Ruthie replied. "And so was getting Kevin to propose to you in the first place."

"Let's not go down that particular road right now," Mrs. Camden warned.

"And then Dad almost wouldn't marry you because he wanted to quit the church," Simon added.

Lucy shook her head at the memory. "There was a moment back then when I thought Dad was only going back to the church to marry Kevin and me."

"That wasn't the case and you know

it!" said Reverend Camden from the doorway.

"Dad!" Lucy jumped up and hugged her father.

"What's all this, then?" asked the reverend.

Mrs. Camden kissed her husband hello.

"Lucy got her wedding pictures back from Mr. Fuller," she explained. "We were about to look at them."

"Then I'm right on time," Reverend Camden said, snatching a cookie from the tray. But Mrs. Camden was quicker and grabbed it out of his hand.

"I have some nice freshly baked fat-free cookies in the kitchen," she said, wagging her finger at her husband. "I'll get you some, and some caffeine-free tea, too."

"Thanks, honey . . . I guess," said Reverend Camden, frowning.

While they waited for Mrs. Camden to return, Lucy gazed at the photograph taken in front of the church as the family members filed in for the wedding rehearsal.

*The weather certainly was horrid,* Lucy recalled. Even the photograph looked murky, with the glow from the Glenoak Community Church's windows barely visible in the rain and haze.

As she stared at the picture, Lucy's mind wandered back to the night before her wedding, to the rehearsal at her father's church. . . .

# THREE

It was a dark and stormy night—one of the darkest and stormiest that Glenoak had ever seen. The rain came down in buckets, lightning flashed, and thunder rumbled.

Despite the tempest, or maybe because of it, the interior of the Glenoak Community Church felt all the more festive and bright, with candles burning and colorful wedding decorations adorning pews and doorways.

Lucy Camden and Kevin Kinkirk stood at the front of the church, along with Simon and Ruthie. They listened as Reverend Camden explained their roles in the coming ceremony once again.

"Then I pronounce you husband and wife," he said, "and then I tell Kevin that he may kiss the bride, and then I present you both to the church. . . ."

Lucy barely heard her father's words. She was gazing at her husband-to-be with adoring eyes. He was staring back just as adoringly. Then suddenly Lucy's concentration was broken by something her father said.

". . . Kevin and Lucy will proceed down the aisle, and this time Ruthie and Simon follow you, hopefully along with Matt and Mary, then Kevin's sister, Patty Mary, with his brother, Ben. . . ."

"But what if the storm keeps Matt and Mary and Kevin's mom and Patty Mary and Ben from getting here?" Lucy asked.

Kevin touched her shoulder and said, "The airport will open up tomorrow. It has to."

"What if it's just us?" Ruthie asked Kevin. "What if your family doesn't make it?"

Kevin smiled. "As of tomorrow, my family is Lucy and me."

Lucy's heart melted. "I feel like the luckiest woman in the entire world."

"Yes," Kevin teased. "You are."

"I think both of you are very lucky to have found each other," said Reverend Camden.

Lucy looked lovingly at her fiancé. "So we're really going to do this?" she asked, almost disbelieving. "I'm really going to be Mrs. Kevin Kinkirk?"

"You still have doubts about me even now?" asked Kevin.

Lucy grabbed Kevin's wrists and gave him one of her deliberate looks. "Promise me you'll be here," she said. "Promise me you won't leave me at the altar. Promise me that nothing will keep you from marrying me—that neither rain nor snow nor heat nor gloom of night will keep you from your appointed rounds."

Kevin reached out and stroked Lucy's face. "I promise," he whispered.

Then Kevin took Lucy into his arms and kissed her. But as she kissed him back, a sudden crack of thunder announced the presence of a visitor. As if by magic, Colonel Camden's elderly housekeeper, Gabrielle, appeared at the back of the church.

Eccentric as always, Gabrielle was dressed like Mary Poppins, with hat askew on top of a woolly head of graying hair, a long raincoat, and an umbrella in her wrinkled hand. With her quiet way of making an entrance and her wild, weird stare, the woman's sudden arrival startled everyone in the church.

"Am I too late?" Gabrielle cried.

"Too late for the wedding?" Reverend Camden replied. "No. But we just finished the rehearsal."

"The Colonel sent me," Gabrielle explained, referring to Reverend Camden's ex-Marine father and Lucy's grandfather.

"Because of the weather, the Colonel isn't going to make it," Gabrielle informed them. "So I'm here to help in any way I can."

Mrs. Camden stepped forward. "I'm sorry you drove all the way from wherever you drove," she said. "But I don't think there's anything you can do, Gabrielle. But you're welcome to come to the wedding, of course."

"Not unless I can make a contribution

in some way," Gabrielle declared. "I insist on helping."

Reverend Camden and his wife exchanged glances.

"Really, we're happy to have you," Reverend Camden said. "But other than showing up at seven-thirty tomorrow night and having a good time, there's nothing you can do."

Gabrielle stared at them for a long moment.

"I'll call the Colonel and let him know," Gabrielle finally announced. It sounded like a threat more than a promise. With that, Gabrielle turned and left the church.

"I hope that wasn't a bad omen," Ruthie whispered to Simon, who nodded.

At the front of the church, Kevin turned to Lucy. "What was that?" he asked.

Lucy frowned. "I'm not sure."

Suddenly another crash of thunder seemed to shake the very foundations of the Glenoak Community Church.

That night, Lucy tossed and turned. Too tense to sleep, she rubbed her tired eyes, sat up, and glanced at the clock: 2:00 A.M.

Lucy sighed. "Unless I'm crazy, it was two o'clock the last time I checked this stupid clock."

Lucy stared at the clock for ten whole seconds. The second hand didn't move. She reached out and flipped the switch on the lamp next to her bed.

No light. Nada. Not even one little watt.

"Great!" she cried. "The electricity's out! How can I get married in a church with no lights?"

Ready to scream with frustration, Lucy glanced at Ruthie in the next bed. The girl was sound asleep.

Lucy tossed the sheets aside, shoved her arms into her robe, and walked out of the room.

Mere seconds after Lucy departed, Ruthie opened her eyes and saw the empty bed next to hers. Rising quickly, Ruthie threw on her own robe and left the room, too—in search of the bride-to-be.

Lucy, meanwhile, had tiptoed across the hall to Ruthie's room, where Kevin was spending the night. Tapping the door lightly, she put her head against the jamb and called, "Kevin? It's me."

Not a sound came from behind Kevin's door. But in his own bedroom, Simon sat up and listened.

"Kevin?" Lucy called, a little louder. "We have to talk."

In the Camdens' bedroom, a worried Mrs. Camden nudged her husband.

"I'm awake," Reverend Camden whispered, staring at the dark ceiling. "I heard her."

Impatient, Lucy turned the knob and pushed the door open. "Kevin!" she rasped, a little louder now.

Inside the bedroom, Kevin opened his eyes with a start. He sat up. "Lucy?" he whispered, smiling when he saw his fiancée creeping across the room in her robe.

"Hi," Lucy said.

"Hi, yourself," Kevin replied. "Can't wait until tomorrow night?"

Lucy frowned. "I'm scared," she admitted.

"Of me?"

"Of the wedding! What if no one makes it?"

Kevin laughed.

"Shhh!" Lucy hissed. "Someone will hear you."

But it was already too late for that. Outside in the hallway, Ruthie, Simon, and Lucy's parents had gathered. All of them were straining to hear what was going on inside Ruthie's old room.

"Did Lucy say anything to you?" whispered Reverend Camden to Ruthie, who shook her head.

"Not a word."

"Do you think she'll call it off?" Simon asked.

"No!" said Mrs. Camden with more certainty than she actually felt.

Simon scratched his head. "Then what are they doing in there?"

Just then they heard Kevin laugh. Lucy squealed, then giggled.

"Shhhhhhh!" they heard Lucy say. Inside the bedroom, Lucy covered her mouth to squelch an outburst of laughter.

"What did you think?" Kevin demanded as he pulled the sheets up to his chin. "I was going to be wearing my pajamas and a smoking jacket? I didn't know you were going to wake me up in the middle of the night."

Lucy backed away from the bed. "Put something on," she said. "I'll step out into the hall and wait for you."

Then Lucy opened the door—and got a big surprise. "What are you doing here!" she cried to her family in the hallway.

"We might ask you the same thing," Reverend Camden replied, folding his arms across his chest.

"I wanted to talk to Kevin about whether or not we should go through with the wedding," said Lucy, "considering no one can get here and it's still storming."

Lucy pointed to the flashlight her father was clutching in one hand. "The electricity went out!" she exclaimed. "How can we have a wedding without electricity?"

"I'm sure it's just temporary," Reverend Camden reassured her as he said a quick slient prayer and tried the hall light switch. It didn't work. "The electricity will come back on in a few minutes," he said, "maybe an hour at most."

"But who knows when it will go out

again!" cried Lucy. "And who wants to get married in the dark?"

Just then, Kevin stepped into the hallway, wearing worn sweatpants and a T-shirt. He halted in surprise when he saw the crowd gathered outside the bedroom door.

"I didn't realize everyone was waiting for me," Kevin said, blushing.

"They're not!" Lucy declared. "They're going back to bed."

Ruthie stood firm. "Without knowing whether or not you're calling off the wedding? I don't think so."

Kevin looked at Lucy. "We're not calling off the wedding," he stated.

"But the weatherman said that it's supposed to rain again tomorrow night," Lucy pointed out. "And even if the airport opens, it's been closed for more than twenty-four hours. The flights are going to be backed up."

Kevin opened his mouth to speak, then closed it again. He turned to face the Camdens. "Do you mind?" he asked.

Reverend Camden shrugged. Mrs. Camden nodded and pushed Ruthie along. In a few moments, the hallway was empty. Kevin and Lucy were alone.

"Now what's this all about?" Kevin asked.

"Let's go back inside, where we can get some privacy," Lucy said, pushing open the door to Ruthie's old bedroom.

"Privacy?" Kevin looked at his bride-to-be doubtfully. "In this family?"

# FOUR

Back inside Ruthie's old bedroom, Kevin kissed Lucy.

"Still have doubts about me?" he asked in a whisper.

"I have doubts about the storm letting up, not us!" Lucy said, not being entirely honest.

Kevin took Lucy's hand in his. "As much as I wanted my mom and Ben and Patty Mary to be at my wedding, if they're not there, I'll be okay."

"But I want my grandparents and Matt and Mary to be there," Lucy insisted.

Kevin moved to kiss her again, but Lucy pulled back. "On second thought," she added, "I don't want them there so much that I would want to wait." Lucy smiled. And this time, she kissed Kevin.

"We could just delay it for twenty-four hours," Lucy suggested.

"We could," Kevin replied with a curt nod. "But who knows if given another day, our families can get in? And when the airport does open, I'm hoping we can get out—to our honeymoon."

"It's just that I want everything to be perfect," Lucy said with a sigh. "Even though I know life's not perfect."

"No, it's not," Kevin agreed. Then he took Lucy in his arms again.

She smiled. "But parts of life are very, very good. . . ."

After the unexpected family meeting in the dimly lit hallway, Reverend and Mrs. Camden decided on a strategy of divide and conquer. That way, each of them could deal with any potential crisis that might arise during the night.

Mrs. Camden moved in with Lucy and Ruthie, while Simon decided to sack out with his father in his parents' bedroom.

Unable to fall asleep, Simon stared at the ceiling. Minutes passed and the house got quiet again. Reverend Camden was just nodding off to sleep when Simon spoke.

"I don't think they'll call off the wedding," he blurted.

Reverend Camden's eyes opened.

"No," he said, sitting up. "Once these things are in motion, they're pretty difficult to stop, although I have had a few couples back out at the very last minute."

Simon continued to stare intently at the ceiling.

"If they call it off, your first official act in the church will be to announce that your daughter's wedding is canceled."

Reverend Camden winced. "That wouldn't be good," he said.

"No," Simon agreed.

For Eric Camden, things had been hard since his heart bypass operation. Though Reverend Camden had returned to his church duties—with the help of a young minister named Chandler Hampton—he had yet to perform an important church ceremony like a wedding. In fact, his daughter's wedding was to be his first since returning from his illness.

Suddenly David and Sam burst into the room. The twin little boys had pulled their little black tuxedo jackets on over their pajamas.

"Is it time to get up?" asked David.

"Is it morning?" asked Sam.

"Is Lucy getting married?" the twins asked together.

Reverend Camden smiled and stifled a yawn. "It's the middle of the night, guys," he told them. "Go back to bed."

But the twin boys just stood in the doorway, waiting.

"I don't want to hurt anyone's feelings," said Simon, "but you boys should really go back to your room."

Blinking, Sam and David didn't move.

Finally Simon shrugged and looked at his father. Reverend Camden shook his head, then patted the bed. The twins happily ran over and hopped on.

With good-nights all around, Simon closed his eyes and tried once again to sleep.

Meanwhile, in Lucy's bedroom, Mrs. Camden sat with Ruthie on the second bed, impatiently waiting for Lucy to finish her talk with Kevin and return to her own bedroom.

"What happens if she doesn't come back soon?" Ruthie asked.

"Then I'll go get her," Mrs. Camden replied. "It's late. We all have a big day tomorrow. This is no time for cold feet—or anything else."

Ruthie made a face. "When I get married, I'm going to elope."

"No, you are not!" Mrs. Camden declared. "I want to be there. Your father wants to be there. Your brothers and sisters want to be there, too."

"Okay," Ruthie said, throwing up her hands. "You and Dad can be the two witnesses when I elope. But everyone else can forget it."

"Ruthie, marriage is about family," said Mrs. Camden softly. "Don't you want your family—your entire family—to be there?"

"They would still be my family whether or not they're at my wedding," Ruthie replied.

Mrs. Camden frowned. "You're getting married in your father's church by your father, and all your brothers and your sisters will be there."

Ruthie rolled her eyes. "Sorry," she said, crossing her arms. "I'm not sure that's in the cards for me. I don't even think it's in the cards for Lucy because I don't think anyone's going to get here for the wedding."

"Don't even say that!" exclaimed Mrs. Camden.

"What? It's not like my saying it is going to keep them away," Ruthie pointed out. "There's a storm. The airport is closed. We have to deal with reality. If Lucy and Kevin want everyone to be there, then they're going to have to delay or even cancel the wedding."

"Hey! Enough, doomsayer," Mrs. Camden said. "Could you try to think pleasant thoughts? Please."

Ruthie was lost in thought for a moment. Then a big grin brightened her face.

Mrs. Camden raised an eyebrow.

"I was just thinking," said Ruthie.

"Yes?"

"I was just thinking that when I do get married, I hope it's to Peter Petrowski."

Mrs. Camden blinked in surprise. Then she smiled. "So you have a little crush on Peter? I didn't think you liked him that much . . . in that way. I thought you were just friends."

Ruthie shook her head. "No," she said. "I think I'm in love."

"Wow," Mrs. Camden said. "You know, I could have waited a day or two after Lucy got married to hear that. . . . But on the other hand, I'm glad you told me. I like Peter. What do you like about him, Ruthie?"

"Everything. Especially when he calls me honey or sweetheart." Ruthie beamed. "That is so cool."

"Yeah. Cool." Mrs. Camden looked at the bedroom door again. No sign of Lucy. She sighed.

After a few more minutes, Mrs. Camden and Ruthie stretched out beside each other on the second bed and closed their eyes.

A little while later, the door opened and Lucy crept quietly into the room. Happy, the family dog, trotted in behind her and sat at the foot of the bed.

With a big smile on her face, Lucy draped her robe over the chair and crawled into her own bed. As she pulled the covers up, a quiet voice came from the darkness.

"Good night," whispered Mrs. Camden.

"Good night," said Ruthie.

"Good night," Lucy said.

They all settled in again, and the room got quiet. Soon everyone in the house was fast asleep.

# FIVE

"Is that a bruise on Chandler's chin?" Reverend Camden asked, lifting a photograph from the stack of pictures spread out on the table.

Then he grabbed the next photograph in the series and studied it. He could see the bruise in that picture, too.

"That *is* a bruise on his chin!" Reverend Camden said, horrified. "Is it possible that my assistant minister was involved in a brawl before he arrived at Lucy's wedding?"

Lucy quickly snatched the pictures away from her father and stuffed them into the album's clear plastic pockets.

"Chandler had a difficult drive, remember, Dad?" Lucy said. "He and Roxanne drove all night to get to Las Vegas in time to bring Kevin's mother and his brother to the wedding."

"That's right. I remember," Reverend Camden said with a snap of his fingers. "But a long drive doesn't explain the bruise on his chin or the scraped knuckles clearly visible in this shot."

Reverend Camden held up the offending photograph.

"Well, at least Mrs. Kinkirk and Ben made it to the wedding," Mrs. Camden said. "Thanks to Chandler and Roxanne."

"Here's a nice picture of Ben," said Mrs. Camden. "He's almost as handsome as Kevin, even though he's not wearing a tuxedo."

"He does look nice," Lucy said, happy to steer the conversation away from Chandler Hampton's bruises. "It's a shame that Ben and Mary didn't get back together."

Then Ruthie and Mrs. Camden launched into a discussion of Mary's ex-boyfriends, which was just fine with Lucy.

Though she didn't want to tell her father all the grisly details, Lucy knew exactly how Chandler got that bruise on his face. And how Roxanne caught the flu, too.

Lucy knew the score because Kevin had heard the story from his mother and his brother, Ben. And since Lucy had become Mrs. Kevin Kinkirk, she'd told her husband that he was compelled by matrimony to tell her everything he knew about what had happened that night. . . .

Thunder rumbled and rain lashed the pavement. Behind the wheel of her police car, Roxanne strained to see the freeway through the darkness, the fog, and the rain-splattered windshield.

She was on hour eleven of what would soon become a twelve-hour shift, and the storm hadn't made her job as a police officer any easier. There had been dozens of accidents all over Glenoak and the surrounding freeways. So far, at least, there had been no serious injuries. Roxanne hoped the community's luck would hold out for the rest of the storm.

A sudden burst of lightning revealed a car on the shoulder of the road just a short distance ahead. As Roxanne slowed down, she could see a single passenger inside. Pulling up behind the disabled vehicle, Roxanne saw the rain was letting up, so she turned off her windshield wipers.

Still behind the wheel of the squad car, she eyed the other car warily. Nighttime stops like this could be dangerous, especially without her partner for backup. With Kevin off getting ready for his wedding the next day, Roxanne was forced to handle this police stop alone.

To be safe, she radioed her position and the license number of the stranded vehicle before she left her squad car. She was somewhat relieved to see the other car had a doctor's license plate. The driver was, presumably, a physician, which would explain why he was out driving on a terrible night like this.

Grabbing a flashlight, Roxanne climbed out of the squad car. Slipping a little on the wet ground, she noticed that the disabled car had both front tires sunk halfway into the mud. This car wasn't going anywhere anytime soon. Warily, Roxanne shone the flashlight on the passenger's face.

"Thank God," said the man with relief.

"I've got to get to the hospital to deliver a baby, and some guy ran me off the road!"

"There are accidents all over the city," said Roxanne. "But we've got a break in the rain for a few minutes. Come on, I'll help you."

The rain had indeed stopped, and the man opened the door and climbed out of his car to inspect the damage. Roxanne recognized him instantly. And he obviously recognized her, too.

"Aren't you . . . ?" said Dr. Hastings.

"Roxanne . . . Kevin's partner," Roxanne said, offering her hand.

"Of course," said Hank, shaking it. "I'm Dr. Hank Hastings. I'm married to Reverend Camden's sister, Julie."

"Right," Roxanne said, nodding. "We met at the house, Christmas."

Roxanne inspected Dr. Hastings's car. Her initial estimation was correct: the sedan was stuck in the mud.

"Lock up your car and come with me. I'll drive you to the hospital."

Roxanne opened the squad car door and reached inside. She lifted the receiver and radioed dispatch again. This time she asked for a tow truck. Then she told the watch captain that she was going to drive the doctor to the hospital.

When Dr. Hastings was in the passenger seat and buckled up, Roxanne got behind the wheel and started the engine. Fishtailing in the mud, the squad car slid onto the road.

Then, with sirens blaring and lights flashing, Roxanne pushed the gas pedal to the floor and raced Dr. Hastings toward Glenoak Hospital.

"Will I see you at the wedding tomorrow?" Roxanne asked over the noise.

Hank Hastings nodded. "If this delivery goes well," he said.

They rode on in silence. A few minutes later, Roxanne delivered Dr. Hastings to the hospital.

"Thanks, Roxanne," Dr. Hastings called over his shoulder as he hurried to the maternity ward. "You may have saved a life tonight—two of them, in fact."

"That's why I do this job," she whispered to herself.

Then, utterly exhausted, she plopped down on a plastic chair and closed her tired eyes. *But only for a moment,* she promised herself.

After twelve hours on duty and maybe four hours of sleep, Roxanne wondered how she would manage to look glamorous for Lucy and Kevin's wedding tomorrow evening. She'd already bought a brand-new gown, with high heels to match, because she wanted to look stunning.

Roxanne rubbed her weary eyes and opened them. Then she rose, shook some of the water off her jacket, and headed outside. But at the front entrance, she froze in her tracks.

"What are you doing here?" Roxanne asked, blinking in surprise.

"I called the station," Reverend Chandler Hampton replied. "The watch captain told me where I could find you."

The young minister studied Roxanne's appearance.

"What happened to you?" he demanded.

"It's been a terrible night," said Roxanne, pushing back her hair.

She didn't like Chandler seeing her like this—after twelve hours on duty in the rain. Then she noticed he wasn't looking so spiffy, either. His hair was mussed, he hadn't shaved, and he was wearing faded jeans and an old jacket.

"I'm afraid it's about to get worse," Chandler said ominously.

Roxanne stared at him, waiting for the bad news.

"Kevin's brother, Ben, called me," Chandler began. "He and Mrs. Kinkirk got a flight to Las Vegas, but now they're stuck. They can't get a rental car because there are no rental cars left. . . ."

Roxanne rolled her eyes. She knew where this conversation was going, and she didn't like it.

"They were going to try to get a flight into a smaller airport tomorrow," Chandler explained, "but they really don't want to risk missing the wedding. . . ."

Chandler's voice trailed off. He was looking at her with those big brown eyes of his.

"So you're going to go pick them up?" said Roxanne, hands on hips.

"I was thinking maybe *we* would go pick them up," Chandler replied hopefully.

"I'm just getting off a twelve-hour shift!" exclaimed Roxanne.

Chandler nodded. "I understand," he said.

Then Roxanne stuck her finger in his

chest. "And you're not driving to Vegas," she declared. "The roads all around Glenoak are terrible!"

Chandler shrugged. "I have to."

"You don't have to!"

Chandler said nothing for a long moment. Then they both looked at their watches.

"Even if we leave right now . . ." Roxanne's voice trailed off when she saw the determination in Chandler's eyes—those big beautiful brown eyes.

"I'll call the watch captain and tell him I'm off duty. Then we can get started," Roxanne said, surrendering.

"You drive tonight while I sleep," she continued. "Then I'll drive on the way back to Glenoak. I think I can handle the drive across the desert after a couple of hours of beauty sleep."

"You don't need it!" said Chandler with a grin. "You're beautiful already."

Smiling, Roxanne took Chandler's hand in hers, and they were off. . . .

# SIX

*At least it isn't raining in the desert,* Roxanne thought hours later as she clutched her aching stomach in the backseat of Chandler's car. She tried to open her eyes, but the brilliant sunlight seemed to stab directly into her brain. She was hurting all over and she felt queasy. Ben Kinkirk was driving and he'd already stopped the car twice so she could be sick.

"I must have caught something during my shift yesterday," she moaned. *And driving to Las Vegas and back hasn't helped, either,* she thought.

"How are you feeling?" Chandler asked, sitting beside her. He placed his cool hand on her hot forehead.

45

"My head is killing me," she said. "But at least I don't feel like throwing up anymore. . . . Not that there's anything left down there to throw up."

"Take it easy," Chandler said quietly. "Ben is driving, and we should be in Glenoak in four or five hours."

"Maybe you should try to drink something," said Mrs. Kinkirk, a tall, attractive blonde wearing elegant clothes. She sat in the front seat beside Ben.

Roxanne nodded and took a tiny sip from the bottled water.

"Drink some more," Mrs. Kinkirk insisted.

Roxanne drank a little deeper, then swallowed three large gulps. She instantly regretted it.

"Pull over!" she cried, covering her mouth.

"I see a gas station up ahead," Ben said, turning the wheel. "Don't throw up in the backseat. Please!"

"Hey!" Chandler cried. "It's my car. Roxanne can throw up in the backseat if she wants to."

A moment later, the car skidded to a halt in front of a seedy restroom at a run-down roadside gas station. Roxanne was out the door and in the ladies' room in a flash. Chandler followed her, stopping at the restroom door.

"I'm going to get something to eat," Ben announced. Five minutes later, he returned with an armful of food from the gas station's vending machines. He tore open a bag of corn chips and dumped them into his mouth.

"Want some?" he asked with his mouth full, thrusting the bag at his mother. With a wrinkled nose, Mrs. Kinkirk waved him off.

Then Ben climbed behind the wheel of Chandler's car, eating an ice cream cone.

"You're going to be sick, too, if you keep eating like that," Mrs. Kinkirk said.

Just then, Roxanne stumbled out of the ladies' room, startled to find Chandler waiting for her there.

"You were standing out here listening to me puking?" she moaned.

"You look terrible," Chandler cried.

"Oh God," Roxanne gasped. "You heard me?"

"It's okay," said Chandler, taking her

hand. "But I think we'd better get you to a hospital."

"We have to get to that wedding," Roxanne said. "If I'm not at Lucy and Kevin's wedding, I'm dead."

Roxanne stumbled away from Chandler, dying of embarrassment under her sickly pallor. "I can't believe you were just standing there listening. . . ."

Chandler led her back to the car. "I really think you should go to a hospital. There must be a hospital somewhere."

"I'm not going to a hospital," Roxanne said stubbornly. Then she climbed into the backseat and covered her eyes. Chandler climbed in beside her.

"We have to get her to a hospital," he said to Ben.

"We'll drop you off," Ben replied.

"Ben!" Mrs. Kinkirk cried, slapping her son's arm.

"What?" said Ben. "We're never going to get to this wedding with her stopping at every other gas station."

"I'll remind you again, it's my car," said Chandler.

"So you should stay with us when we dump her at the emergency ward."

With that, Ben took a big bite out of his ice cream cone. Roxanne took one look at him chewing his food and bolted out of the car again.

Watching her go, Chandler blew his top—in a polite, controlled manner, of course.

"Mrs. Kinkirk," he said. "I apologize in advance for anything I do to Ben."

Then Chandler turned to Ben, his eyes steely. "Get out of the car!" he commanded.

"Why?" asked Ben with a smirk.

Jaw clenched, Chandler replied, "Because I am going to kill you."

Ben snorted. "You're a man of God. You can't kill me."

"You never heard of the Crusades? The Inquisition?"

Ben rolled his eyes. "You're not a Catholic."

"Boys!" Mrs. Kinkirk cried.

But when she saw the fury in their faces, she fled. "I'll check on Roxanne."

"No," Chandler replied. "I'll check on Roxanne."

When he was gone, Ben turned to his mother. "Can't we just leave them here?"

"No, we can't."

"Why not?"

"Because they drove all the way to Vegas to pick us up. And she's a police officer. She'd have us arrested."

"Oh, all right," Ben said.

Roxanne returned to the car with Chandler. She climbed into the seat and leaned against the door.

"I really think we should forget the wedding at this point," Chandler insisted. "We should just get you to a hospital."

Roxanne looked up at Chandler, her eyes pleading. "I have to get to that wedding. I *have* to!"

"No, you don't have to," Chandler replied. "You're sick. And I'm responsible."

"You're not responsible," Roxanne insisted, clutching his hand. "You didn't make me sick. And if I don't get there, Kevin is going to kill me, so I won't just be sick, I'll be dead."

"Could we please go?" Ben asked impatiently.

Chandler stared at him. "I can't believe I drove all night to pick you up in Las Vegas and now you think we're inconveniencing you?"

Ben got out of the car and stretched. "We could have walked there faster than this."

Chandler threw open the door and jumped out of the car. "I just want to hit you so badly, I can't even tell you."

Ben thrust out his chin and pointed to it. "If we can leave after you hit me, then hit me! Go ahead."

Roxanne stumbled out of the car and put up her hand. "No one is hitting anyone," she said in her official police voice. Then she swayed on her feet and had to clutch the car to steady herself. Covering her mouth, she raced to the ladies' room once more.

Chandler waited for the door to close behind Roxanne; then he punched Ben. Right in the jaw.

A second later, Ben was flat on his back on the pavement and Chandler was diving on top of him, fists swinging.

"Stop it, boys!" yelled Mrs. Kinkirk, jumping out of the car and waving her arms. "Ben, Chandler . . . Please stop!"

But the "boys" ignored her. In a ball of tangled limbs and flashing fists, Chandler and Ben rolled around on the concrete. There were groans of pain and cries of triumph as fists landed.

Then Ben broke free and jumped to his feet. Chandler came up after him. Mrs. Kinkirk threw herself in the middle of the fray.

"Now stop it! Both of you," she cried.

"He started it!" Ben whined.

Chandler rolled his eyes. "What are you, twelve?"

Stepping around Mrs. Kinkirk, Ben smacked Chandler in the face. The minister went down, but he grabbed Ben's shirt on the way and took him down, too! Then they were up on their feet again, fists swinging wildly with few blows finding their targets anymore.

Just then, Roxanne rushed out of the restroom.

"Stop or I'll shoot!" she cried.

Both men stopped fighting and stared at her.

"You have a gun?" Ben asked incredulously.

"Yes, I have a gun!" Roxanne replied.

"With you?" Chandler asked.

Roxanne looked at Chandler, then down at her belt. "Uh, no," she said sheepishly.

Chandler went back to swinging at Ben. Ben kicked Chandler's legs out from under him.

Roxanne and Mrs. Kinkirk looked at each other.

"If it were Ben and Kevin, I'd just leave them here," said Mrs. Kinkirk.

"If I were feeling better, I'd join them," said Roxanne.

"What does that mean?" demanded Mrs. Kinkirk.

"That means that Ben has been nothing but rude and inconsiderate since he got in this car," Roxanne replied.

"He's tired," Mrs. Kinkirk said angrily. "We've been up for almost seventy-two hours and he'd been at a fire the night before we left."

"So you're just going to make excuses for him?" asked Roxanne, glancing at Ben and Chandler, still wrestling on the ground.

Mrs. Kinkirk frowned. "You want a piece of me?"

"I'm a cop!" said Roxanne.

"And I'm a mother of two boys," Mrs. Kinkirk said. "I can beat you up."

Roxanne gave Mrs. Kinkirk a once-over, then announced, "You're dreaming."

Mrs. Kinkirk just shook her head. "I don't think so. . . ."

"I'm sick," Roxanne said, clutching her stomach. "I'm very, very sick. Otherwise I'd fight you."

When they heard those words, Ben and Chandler stopped fighting. Actually, Chandler stopped. Ben was already pinned and helpless.

"Excuse me," Chandler said. "What is going on here?"

Roxanne pulled off her jacket and rolled up her sleeves.

"What the heck?" she said, smirking confidently. "It's me and you, Chandler, against the Kinkirks."

But as Mrs. Kinkirk and Roxanne squared off, Ben broke free of Chandler's grip and ran between them.

"Don't you touch my mother!" Ben cried.

Chandler got into Ben's face. "Your mother is nuts," he said.

Ben threw up his hands. "And your girlfriend is . . . Your girlfriend is . . ."

"It's not a battle of wits, Ben!" cried Mrs. Kinkirk, fists raised. "Let's go for it."

And they did.

# SEVEN

"Here's a cute picture," said Ruthie.

She held up a photograph of Gabrielle and Grandpa Charles sitting together at one of the reception tables. Grandpa Charles was smiling. Gabrielle was staring wide-eyed at the camera.

"Your grandfather looks so handsome in this picture," Mrs. Camden said. "Too bad Ginger couldn't come, too."

"Couldn't . . . or wouldn't?" asked Simon.

"Mostly wouldn't," Mrs. Camden confessed. "It was nice of the Colonel to send Gabrielle to pick up Grandpa and Ginger. But I can't blame Ginger for refusing to get into any vehicle that has Gabrielle behind the wheel."

"Yeah, I hear she's a real terror on the road," said Ruthie, chuckling.

"Now, now, Ruthie. No gossiping," Mrs. Camden chided.

"I'm only repeating what I heard," Ruthie said defensively.

"And that's gossip," said Reverend Camden.

"Well, it sure was lucky Gabrielle was there to help," said Mrs. Camden. "Or Grandpa Charles wouldn't have made it to the wedding at all."

"But you insisted at the time that Gabrielle was a bad omen," said Reverend Camden. "Remember? That night when she showed up at the rehearsal?"

"That wasn't me," Mrs. Camden replied. "That was Ruthie."

"Let's face it," said Lucy. "We all thought Gabrielle's arrival was a bad omen. But if I really cared about bad omens, I would never have gotten married in the first place. I mean, how many brides have to contend with storms, a power failure, a leaky roof, and the arrival of Gabrielle—all on their wedding day?"

"True," said Ruthie.

Lucy smiled. "Let's just say that if I

really believed in bad omens, I would still be single."

"These pictures of the reception are nice," Reverend Camden observed.

Mrs. Camden nodded. "Everyone looks like they're having fun."

Then she held up another photo. "Tell me if this isn't the best picture yet?"

Mrs. Camden displayed a photograph of the entire wedding party, all lined up in front of the cake in a perfect wedding-picture pose.

"Considering what happened at the reception, we were lucky to get that particular shot!" said Simon.

"I'll say," said Ruthie.

"That is a wonderful shot." Lucy sighed. "I want to have it framed. Just to remind me of the day when my whole family came together for my wedding."

"Yeah," said Ruthie. "And to remind you of what the cake looked like before Ben got to it!"

"Now, Ruthie," Reverend Camden cautioned. "Accidents will happen."

"It's hard to believe that only a few hours before that picture was taken, you gave up hope of anyone showing up for your wedding," said Ruthie.

"Too true," Lucy replied, remembering. . . .

Lucy had been too nervous to eat breakfast the day of her wedding. After a quick shower, she went straight to the attic bedroom to get ready for the ceremony.

Her hair was in curlers and she had just finished applying eye makeup when she saw her father lingering in the hallway, staring at her.

"Dad?" said Lucy.

Reverend Camden remained frozen in place. On his face was a half smile and a faraway gaze.

"Dad!" Lucy said, louder this time.

Reverend Camden blinked, then focused on his daughter.

"Hi," he said.

"Are you okay?" Lucy asked.

"Oh, yeah, I'm fine," said Reverend Camden. "I guess I was just remembering the past."

Then Reverend Camden cleared his throat. "The airport is still closed because of flooding," he told Lucy. "But the good news is that some of the surrounding airports an hour or so away have opened, so there's still hope."

"Good," Lucy said, determined to put her best foot forward. "Then I have hope."

Reverend Camden didn't move.

"Is there anything else?" Lucy asked.

"No, nothing else," he replied. "I was just remembering you . . . as a little girl. You grew up so fast."

Lucy saw the tear in her father's eye and she rose and hugged him.

"Thank you for marrying us," she said. "And thank you for coming back to the church. We all missed you."

Soon Lucy had a tear in her eye, too. Reverend Camden offered her a handkerchief.

"I'm going to be fine," Lucy insisted, wiping her eyes. "I really love Kevin and he's a good man. I'm marrying Kevin because I want to."

"I know," Reverend Camden said.

They hugged again, and then Reverend Camden asked, "Is there anything at all I can do to help today? Beyond marrying you, of course."

Lucy laughed. "Well," she began. "Since it's bad luck for the groom to see the bride before the ceremony, I was wondering . . ."

"If I could get Kevin out of the house?" Reverend Camden guessed. "I'm sure I can arrange that."

After her breakfast, Ruthie found Simon and Kevin watching cartoons.

"Shouldn't you guys be dressed by now?" she asked.

Kevin shook his head. "I'm staying in sweats until I put on my tux."

"I'm doing the same thing," said Simon.

"Have you heard from Ben and your mom?" Ruthie asked Kevin.

"No," he replied. "But I know Ben, and if it takes planes, trains, and automobiles to get them here, they'll get here."

"And if they don't?"

Kevin thought about Ruthie's question for a moment. Then he turned to Simon.

"Hey," he said. "If for any reason my brother doesn't get here, would you be my best man?"

Simon was surprised. "Really?"

"After all," Kevin continued, "we become brothers today."

"But what if Matt gets here and Ben doesn't?"

Kevin shrugged. "I hardly know Matt. . . . So would you do it? If Ben doesn't make it."

"Absolutely," Simon replied. "But as honored as this makes me feel, I still hope Ben makes it here on time."

Minutes later, the phone rang. Reverend Camden answered in his bedroom.

"Just tell me you're coming to Lucy's wedding, no matter who you are," he said into the receiver.

"Eric?" asked Hank Hastings from the other end of the line.

"Hank? Is that you?"

"I'm at the hospital," Dr. Hastings explained. "I've got a difficult delivery going on here and . . . well . . ."

"No one can get into the airports," Reverend Camden said desperately. "You have to come, and you have to bring my sister and my niece and nephew."

"How's three out of four?" Hank asked.

"At the wedding?" asked Reverend Camden hopefully.

"Missing the wedding," Dr. Hastings replied. "We can't bring Erica and the baby out in this weather—they're just getting over a very bad case of the flu. But I promise your sister, Julie, will get there."

"And you?"

"I'm trying," Dr. Hastings explained. "But I can't do a cesarean just because I want to see Lucy and Kevin get married."

Reverend Camden digested the bad news. "Has Julie heard from the Colonel or Ruth?" he asked. "I've been trying to reach them. I want to talk to them."

"They're hiding from you," Hank said. "They said they weren't sure you and Annie liked the wedding gift."

"What wedding gift?"

"Something they call a Gabrielle," Hank replied.

Reverend Camden rolled his eyes. "If you talk to them, tell them we returned her."

Mrs. Camden arrived a moment later.

"Did I just hear the phone?" she asked.

"Hank," Reverend Camden replied.

"Difficult labor at the hospital. He and Julie may or may not make the wedding."

"That's too bad," said Mrs. Camden.

"And by the way, Hank told me Gabrielle was the Colonel's wedding present."

Mrs. Camden shook her head. "Can we send her back?"

Hair still in curlers, Lucy wandered the house until she found her mother in the kitchen, washing dishes.

"Mom?"

Startled, Mrs. Camden turned. Lucy saw tears in her mother's eyes.

"I'm sorry," Mrs. Camden said, brushing them away. "I was just thinking. I wish my dad and Ginger could get here, but . . . mostly I was just missing my mom."

Lucy hugged her mother and held on.

"It's okay," Lucy said. "She's with us because she's part of us always. And you have to be strong, Mom, because . . . well . . ."

Lucy stepped back and grinned. "Because I'm getting married. I'm really getting married."

"I know, I know, Luce," laughed Mrs. Camden. "And I'm so happy for you."

Lucy held up a locket. A very special locket.

"This was Grandma's locket," said Lucy. "You gave it to me on my thirteenth birthday, remember?"

"Of course," said Mrs. Camden. "Is that your something old?"

Lucy nodded. "And the something new is the wedding dress. I just need something borrowed, and the garter will be something blue. Could I borrow some earrings, Mom?"

Mrs. Camden smiled. "Any earrings you want. And thanks for wearing my mother's locket."

Upstairs, Lucy and her mother went through Mrs. Camden's jewelry box. While she tried on various items, Lucy chatted nervously.

"Do you think I'm crazy for going ahead with the wedding even though it looks as if no one is going to get here?" she asked. "It doesn't make me look desperate, does it?"

"No. It doesn't make you look desperate. It was a long shot to get everyone in with the short notice anyway."

Mrs. Camden frowned. "I don't think

my dad and Ginger are going to make it, and we know the Colonel and Ruth and George aren't going to make it."

Lucy lifted an earring to her ear and studied it in the mirror.

"But maybe Matt and Sarah?" she said hopefully.

"They were flying out of New York, too," Mrs. Camden said. "And the flights are stacked up."

"Have you heard from Mary?"

Mrs. Camden shook her head. "Not yet. But maybe she'll get here. After all, she has connections with the airlines."

Lucy tried on another pair of earrings. "Maybe Ben will get here, with Kevin's mom," she said.

"Maybe."

Lucy turned away from the mirror and looked her mother in the eye. "You don't really want me to put off the wedding, do you?"

"No," Mrs. Camden replied. "But if this isn't the right day for you, this is your wedding."

Lucy hugged her mom again. "This is the right day for me."

"Then those earrings look like the best choice to me," said Mrs. Camden.

"I agree," Lucy said with a nod.

"Have you eaten today? Anything at all?"

"No, Mom . . . too nervous."

"Well, I'm going to fix you a sandwich. I don't want you fainting from hunger before you say 'I do.'"

Mrs. Camden arrived in the kitchen in time to hear the telephone. But the twins beat her to answering it.

"Camden residence," Sam and David said together. Then they both screamed with delight.

"Mary!"

Mrs. Camden grabbed the phone. "Mary!" she cried. "Please tell me you're going to get here."

"I've got a rental car and I'm still hours away, but we should make it."

Mrs. Camden frowned. "We?"

She could feel Mary's Cheshire cat grin on the other end of the line. "I'm going to bring someone with me, if it's okay."

"Oh, well, of course you can bring someone with you!" Mrs. Camden said with forced cheerfulness. "Want to tell me who it is?"

Mrs. Camden heard Mary chuckle. "Why don't we just let that be a surprise?"

Before she could get out another word, Mary said, "Bye, Mom."

*Now who could this mystery guest be?* Mrs. Camden wondered.

# EIGHT

Kevin was still lounging on the living room couch watching cartoons when Reverend Camden found him. Simon and Ruthie were nowhere to be seen.

"Where is everybody?" Reverend Camden asked.

"Well, Ruthie said she had to do her hair and her nails before the wedding. And Simon wanted to make a phone call before he got ready. I'm watching television."

"What are you watching?"

"Cartoons."

Reverend Camden sat down on the couch next to Kevin.

"I thought maybe we should talk," Reverend Camden began.

Kevin lifted the remote control and switched off the television.

"You look pretty calm," Reverend Camden observed.

"And how are you?" Kevin asked. "Still a little nervous about returning to your church after being away so long?"

Reverend Camden shrugged. "Actually, I'm okay about that."

"Then you're nervous about your daughter getting married to me?"

Reverend Camden chose his words carefully.

"It's not the wedding ceremony I'm worried about," he said. "It's more . . . well, my daughter."

"Whoa!" Kevin cried. "We're not going to talk about . . . You're not going to . . . This isn't that old-fashioned father-to-future-son-in-law talk, is it?"

Reverend Camden nodded and tried to keep from smirking.

Suddenly Kevin looked at his watch, then jumped to his feet.

"I didn't realize it's so late."

Then, as fast as he could move, Kevin fled the living room.

Not a minute later, Lucy entered, purse over her shoulder and a small suitcase in her hand. Her hair was still in curlers, but she was dressed in jeans and a blouse. She was also wearing her grandmother's locket and a beautiful pair of antique earrings.

"Where's Kevin?"

Reverend Camden smiled. "I got him out of the house, just like you asked."

"You didn't chase him off or anything?"

"Maybe I kind of did," Reverend Camden replied sheepishly. "But in my defense, you said you wanted him out of the house, so I got him out of the house."

"Well," Lucy replied. "Mom's waiting in the car. We're heading down to the church."

"I'll see you there."

"With Kevin?" asked Lucy.

"With Kevin."

Lucy gave her father a hug and a kiss.

"Just curious," she said. "How did you get Kevin out of the house?"

Reverend Camden grinned. "I led him to believe we were about to have a conversation about the wedding night."

Lucy laughed. "Ah. Nice to see you're back on your game."

"So," Reverend Camden said. "Who do you think Mary's bringing?"

"I don't know." Lucy shrugged. "But Mom and I decided we're not going to worry about it."

"How very Zen of you," Reverend Camden replied. "I'm still hoping to hear Matt's on his way."

"I hope so, too," said Lucy. "But if the Colonel couldn't get here, I'm not counting on Matt and Sarah getting here, either. It would be nice, even wonderful, but . . ."

"Yeah." Reverend Camden nodded. "No expectations, no disappointments."

Out in the driveway, Mrs. Camden honked the horn twice.

"Gotta go! Mom's waiting," Lucy called as she hurried out the door. "See you in church, Dad."

Reverend Camden actually gasped in surprise when Ruthie appeared at the top of the stairs. She looked lovely and totally sophisticated in her bridesmaid gown. Even her hair and the touch of makeup she wore—applied carefully by Lucy before she left—were perfect.

"Oh, my," said Reverend Camden.

"Yeah," Ruthie said, beaming. "I do look grown-up, don't I?"

Reverend Camden nodded. "Yes, you do. You look like a young woman, a beautiful young woman."

"Not to worry," Ruthie replied. "Even if I do marry Peter Petrowski, I'm not getting married until I'm thirty."

Reverend Camden blinked. This was the first he'd heard about marriage to Peter!

Ruthie breezed past him and out the front door—but not before picking up a large flat parcel hidden behind the umbrella stand. The parcel was wrapped in plastic to protect it from the rain and to hide the contents.

Reverend Camden was about to ask what the parcel was when he heard a noise at the top of the stairs. He looked up to see Simon waiting there in his tuxedo.

Reverend Camden's heart swelled with pride once more. He brushed away a tear, but not before Simon spotted the gesture.

"You better save those tears for Lucy," he said. "I've got a feeling this is going to be a very weepy wedding."

Simon came down the stairs and Reverend Camden adjusted his tie.

"It's going to be a very happy wedding," he insisted.

Simon rolled his eyes. "We'll see."

Kevin appeared at the top of the stairs next, holding David's hand on one side and Sam's on the other. The twins were decked out in evening clothes, but Reverend Camden was relieved to see that the effect was cute—not at all sophisticated like their older siblings.

"Finally, children who don't look all grown-up," Reverend Camden said with a sigh of relief. Then he glanced at Kevin.

"You're not going to be ready for children for years."

Kevin nodded and grinned. "I know that, Dad."

Reverend Camden hugged his future son-in-law. Ruthie, who had already run outside and tucked the parcel in the backseat of the car, smiled innocently up at Kevin.

"Have you heard from anyone in your family?" she asked.

"My sister called," Kevin said. "The bad news is she can't make it. The good news is she met a guy at the airport."

"How's that good news?" Ruthie asked.

"I met Lucy at the airport in Buffalo," Kevin explained. "Maybe this guy will turn out to be the love of my sister's life."

"And Ben?" Simon asked.

Kevin shrugged. "I haven't heard a word from him," he said. "But he'll probably turn up sometime in the next day or two. You're still my best man."

"I have the ring," Simon announced.

He drew a ring box from his pocket and snapped the lid open. He and Kevin gazed at the wedding band inside. Then Simon closed the box and tucked it back into his jacket.

"All right," said Reverend Camden, clapping. "I've got the best man, the maid of honor, the ring bearers, and the groom, and I'm the minister. We're set to go!"

Just then there was a knock at the front door.

"Mary and the mystery man?" guessed Ruthie.

"Matt and Sarah," Simon said hopefully.

"Ben and my mother," said Kevin.

"Just open the door!" said little Sam.

"Please!" David agreed.

Ruthie grabbed the knob and threw open the front door.

"Hi!" said Cecilia, Simon's date for the wedding. Peter stood next to her. Both were dressed to the nines.

"Wow!" gushed Simon when he saw Cecilia.

"Wow, yourself," said Cecilia when she saw Simon. As they kissed, Peter walked up to Ruthie.

"Honey," he said. "You couldn't look prettier if you were the bride."

Ruthie blushed three shades of red. "Thanks," she said shyly.

Kevin looked at Reverend Camden, who was staring at Simon and Cecilia kissing and Peter and Ruthie walking hand in hand to the car.

"Weddings are tough, aren't they, Reverend?" said Kevin.

Reverend Camden nodded but didn't reply. After a long pause, he began pushing people out the front door.

"Time to go," he said.

# NINE

"Lucy, here's a wedding picture you should definitely frame!" cried Ruthie.

She held up a full-length shot of Kevin and Lucy exchanging rings at the front of the church. Reverend Camden stood between them, smiling with happiness and pride.

"That *is* a nice shot," Simon agreed. "I don't think Dad smiled like that since before he got sick."

Reverend Camden looked at the picture. "I smile like that all the time!"

Everyone laughed.

"Ruthie's right. This is a wonderful picture," Mrs. Camden remarked. "It's especially nice to me because just a half an hour before that picture was taken, I thought the wedding wasn't even going to happen!"

Lucy nodded. "I admit I had second thoughts. Big ones . . ."

"Second thoughts?" Mrs. Camden exclaimed. "Your feet couldn't have been more cold if you were hiking across Antarctica in flip-flops!"

"Hey," Lucy said defensively. "A girl can change her mind, you know."

"Yeah," said Simon. "But think how Kevin would have felt. After you made him promise he wouldn't leave you at the altar, you almost left him."

"I just had a few second thoughts. I probably would have come to my senses on my own," Lucy said.

"And if you hadn't, think what a disaster that would have been for me," teased Reverend Camden. "If you had backed out, my first official act after returning to the church would have been to tell half the congregation that my daughter's wedding was off."

"Well," Mrs. Camden said. "Fortunately you didn't have to make that speech."

"Yeah," said Simon. "I had a feeling

something would go wrong. But I also thought that things would turn out right in the end."

Simon turned to Lucy. "After you lost your nerve, what finally convinced you to get married after all?" he asked.

"I didn't lose my nerve, not exactly," Lucy said. "I just had some last-minute jitters. But Mary's 'mystery guest' finally convinced me to go through with the wedding. . . ."

The day of Lucy's wedding, the Glenoak Community Church's main office doubled as the bride's dressing room.

"Your makeup is perfect and so is your hair," Mrs. Camden declared after a long inspection. "I think it's time to get into your wedding dress."

Mrs. Camden unzipped the long plastic bag hanging on the office's closet door hook. She was ready to pull the dress out when she heard her daughter call to her.

"Mom . . . ," Lucy said weakly.

Mrs. Camden turned to find an anxious expression on her daughter's face.

"I . . . I don't know if I can go through with this," Lucy confessed.

Mrs. Camden stood frozen in place, totally flabbergasted by her daughter's words.

"I'm . . . I'm having second thoughts," Lucy admitted. "I should finish college first. I should work for a while. I should have some money in the bank of my own. I should . . ."

Lucy's mouth snapped shut a moment, and her mother just stared, waiting for her to continue.

"I . . . I should know Kevin better," said Lucy, "and I should know me better. What if this is the wrong thing to do?"

Mrs. Camden, still in shock, wrapped Lucy in her arms and held her close. Lucy hugged her mother; then she pulled away and stepped back.

"I can't get married today," Lucy announced in a voice so cool, calm, and determined it sent Mrs. Camden right out of the room.

Mrs. Camden immediately found her husband, who'd been waiting outside in the hallway. She told him what Lucy had said.

"And the scary thing is, she's not crying," said Mrs. Camden. "Not a tear. She says she just doesn't know if she's doing the right thing."

"Maybe she's got a point," he replied.

"Of course she has a point," Mrs. Camden said, a little too loudly. Simon, who was standing at the other end of the hallway, turned his head at the sound of her voice.

"But I know my daughter," Mrs. Camden continued, talking more softly now. "I'm telling you. This is just a case of cold feet . . . and if she doesn't go through with this wedding, she's not going to be happy with herself tomorrow or the next day or the next week or the next year."

Reverend Camden signaled his wife that she was getting too loud again. Already Simon was moving toward them, his expression curious.

"Lucy loves Kevin," Mrs. Camden said, not caring anymore who heard her. "She wants to be married to Kevin. Talk to her!"

"What's going on?" asked Simon.

"Have Ben and Mrs. Kinkirk made it yet?" she asked, dodging the question.

"No," Simon replied. "But Kevin says we don't have to wait for them."

Simon was about to continue when Ruthie entered the hallway with Sam and David in tow.

"No sign of Matt or Mary or Grandpa Charles or the bad omen," said Ruthie.

"I forgot about Gabrielle," said Mrs. Camden.

"There are no bad omens," Reverend Camden told his wife. "There are just nervous brides."

"What does that mean?" asked Ruthie, sensing trouble.

"Yes, what does that mean?" said a voice from the exit door. Everyone turned at once.

"Mary!" Sam and David shouted.

"Mary!" Reverend Camden cried. "I'm so happy you made it."

"Thanks," said Mary, hugging her dad. Since she had just come from the airport, she was still wearing her flight attendant's uniform.

"Oh, this is wonderful," said Mrs. Camden, hugging her eldest daughter.

"Hi, Mom," said Mary. Then she hugged Simon and Ruthie.

"It's great to see you," said Simon.

"And you," Mary replied. "You're looking—"

"Grown-up?" said Simon.

"Distinguished," Mary declared. "And very handsome."

"I hope you didn't come all this way for nothing," Ruthie said. "We've got a nervous bride."

Mary looked at Reverend Camden. Then at Mrs. Camden. They both looked seriously worried. Mary knew at once that they had a problem.

"It's going to be fine," Mrs. Camden insisted. "It has to be fine."

The door to the church office opened a crack. Lucy peeked out and saw Mary.

"Oh, Mary!" Lucy said as they both hugged.

"Hey, what are you so nervous about?" Mary demanded.

"I don't know," Lucy said with a shake of her head. "I just don't know. . . . I don't know anything." Then Lucy hugged Mary again and asked, "So?"

"So what?" Mary replied.

"So where's your mystery date?"

Lucy looked down the hallway, but she saw no new or exotic faces.

Mary just smiled. Then she cupped her mouth and called loudly, "Hey, you!"

Everyone stared nervously down the hallway—until a familiar face appeared around the corner.

"Are you looking for me?" asked Matt Camden.

Reverend and Mrs. Camden ran to greet their married son. Matt looked very different from the last time the family had seen him. His long, shaggy hair had been cut very short. But there were other changes, too. His face appeared older, his expression more certain. Reverend Camden thought that Matt was beginning to look like the physician he was working so hard to become.

"You made it!" said Ruthie.

Lucy threw her arms around her big brother's neck. "I love you!" she cried.

"We've missed you," said Reverend Camden.

"I've missed you, too," said Matt.

"I got him the last seat on the flight I was on," Mary explained.

Lucy frowned, sorry Matt's wife wasn't traveling with him. "So Sarah isn't going to make it?"

"No," Matt said. "But from what I was hearing down the hall, maybe she's not going to be missing anything."

Matt took Lucy by the hand. "Come on. We'll talk."

Leading her inside the church office, Matt turned in the doorway and faced everyone.

"We'll see you upstairs," he told them. "Everything is going to be fine."

The whole Camden family stood frozen, not sure what to do.

"Do what your doctor tells you!" Matt said in a commanding tone. "Go! Be gone! Away!"

Matt shut the door and turned to his sister.

"So," he said, smiling proudly. "My little sister is getting married."

"Maybe," said Lucy doubtfully.

"Sit down," Matt commanded. "We're going to talk. . . ."

# TEN

As she crossed the Glenoak Community Church parking lot, Mrs. Kinkirk adjusted her rumpled outfit. It was then she noticed a dark oil stain on her sleeve—no doubt a result of the wrestling match with Roxanne at that gas station in Nevada!

"How are we going to explain this?" Mrs. Kinkirk moaned to her son, who was limping along beside her.

Ben shrugged. "I guess we'll have to go with the truth, or the cop and the preacher will rat us out."

Inside the church, Ruthie spied the new arrivals. She hurried up to Kevin to deliver the good news. "Your mother and brother are here!"

Kevin rushed to the door to greet them.

"Kevin!" Mrs. Kinkirk called. "We made it, honey."

"Yeah, we made it," said Ben.

As Kevin hugged his mother, Ben glanced around the entryway of the church. He was hoping to see Mary Camden. Ben had dated Mary for a short time, but things hadn't worked out between them. He planned to change that. He wanted a second chance with Mary. He figured this wedding would be his big opportunity to make that happen.

When Kevin finished hugging his mother, he gave his brother a closer look. The smudges of dirt and rumpled clothes weren't exactly menswear chic. He glanced back at his mother—she didn't look much better. Her clothes were wrinkled, her hair was mussed, and there were stains on her sleeves.

"What happened to you two?" he asked.

"We got into a fight," Ben said, rolling his eyes.

"A fight with . . . ?"

"That Hampton boy," Mrs. Kinkirk said. "And his girlfriend."

Kevin blinked. "You two got into a fight with Chandler and Roxanne?"

"Kind of," said Ben.

"Don't worry about it," Mrs. Kinkirk told Kevin. "We won and we're here."

*My mother and my brother, in a fight with my father-in-law's assistant minister and my policewoman partner? On the day of my wedding? Kevin thought. What else can go wrong?*

"Hey!" Simon said, approaching the group. "You made it!"

Simon reached inside his cleaned and pressed tuxedo jacket and pulled out the ring box. He was ready to hand it over to Ben Kinkirk, along with the best man duties. But Kevin stopped him.

With one last disgusted look at his younger brother's soiled, wrinkled clothes, Kevin told Ben, "Simon will be my best man."

"Okay," said Ben. "But I still get to stand up front, right?"

"I guess." Kevin shrugged.

"Let Ben stand up front," Mrs. Kinkirk insisted. "He's your brother."

Kevin nodded and Ben smiled.

"Come on, follow me," said Kevin. "I'll take you somewhere so you can wash up. That must have been some victory."

As the Kinkirks entered the church, Roxanne and Chandler Hampton were crossing the parking lot. Though they sported a few bumps and bruises, they were both cheerful. Roxanne even felt a little bit better, and Chandler had a big smile on his face.

"I can't believe we beat them up," he crowed. "I never get to beat anyone up. I'm a minister."

Then he looked at Roxanne. She still seemed flushed.

"Are you okay?" Chandler asked. "Or should I bring a bucket in?"

"I'm fine," said Roxanne.

"Hey, look, Julie!" said Dr. Hank Hastings to his wife. "Here's the policewoman who rescued me from the side of the road last night."

Julie Hastings turned. "Roxanne! Chandler!" she cried. "You look terrible. Is everything okay?"

"Yes," said Hank. "You both look like heck."

Dr. Hastings took an extralong look at Roxanne. "But you look worse than he does. Are you running a fever? Coming down with the flu?"

"Both of our children are home with the flu," said Julie Hastings. "They've had it for days."

Shooting Dr. Hastings a nasty look, Roxanne cried, "Your children have the flu? . . . So last night, when I stopped to help you, you . . . You carrier, you! You gave me the flu!"

Roxanne was mad enough to spit. Chandler Hampton held her back. "Sorry, Dr. Hastings," he said. "It's been a long day. We'll see you inside."

Rozanne strained against Chandler's grip, and Dr. Hastings and his wife scurried into the aisle to find a seat.

"You better just let it go," Chandler said. "We don't have another fight in us."

Meanwhile, inside the church office, Lucy and Matt sat side by side on Reverend Camden's couch. Matt had listened while Lucy unloaded everything—all her worries, all her fears. She knew Matt would have a solution. She trusted her older brother more than just about anyone. She knew he wouldn't steer her wrong.

"Life is short, Luce," Matt said in a soft voice. "I see it every day. People who thought they'd have more time to do the things they want to do. People who want the ideal and who never appreciated the less-than-ideal ordinary day with their family and friends."

Lucy had to admit she had spent much of her life holding out for the ideal—which was probably why she was so often dissatisfied.

"Since starting medical school, I've seen people who were indecisive or too scared to do what was in their heart," Matt continued. "And then they found out that they weren't going to get another chance—that it was too late."

Lucy knew she didn't want to let her life pass her by. She had too much love to give, and too many things to do, to risk losing it all because she was too afraid to try.

"Your whole life is in front of you," Matt said, taking his sister's hand. "And you've got a man you love to share it with. A man who loves you and wants to share his life with yours." Matt's voice grew more intense as he spoke, and his eyes grew sad, too. "Do you know how many husbands and wives aren't in love with each other? How many people never find someone?"

Lucy frowned and nodded.

"You and Kevin found each other," Matt told her. "You're madly in love with each other. It doesn't matter that it's not exactly as you planned, that it happened before you reached every goal you have."

Matt squeezed Lucy's hand. "You'll still reach your goals. You'll just have someone to hold your hand and encourage you along the way."

Lucy smiled. Matt's words had melted her fears. Only her love for Kevin remained.

"Embrace this experience," Matt said, still clutching her hand. "Get married. Live your life. Be happy."

Matt released Lucy's hand and she hugged him.

"There's only one last problem," she told him.

"What's that?"

"I'm going to need some help zipping up my dress."

Matt laughed. "I can do that," he said.

A few minutes later, Matt slipped out of the church office and spotted his mother in the hallway. He gave her a thumbs-up sign and Mrs. Camden's shoulders slumped in relief.

Five minutes later, the organ began to play. Simon ushered Mrs. Camden to her seat, then took his place beside Kevin and Reverend Camden, who were already standing at the altar.

As Mrs. Camden was about to settle into her pew, she felt herself missing her father and her late mother terribly. A moment later, she heard the gravelly voice of an old woman in her ear.

"Aren't you going to thank me?"

Mrs. Camden turned to find Gabrielle behind her. Next to Gabrielle sat her father!

"Hi, honey, I made it," Grandpa Charles said with a grin.

Mrs. Camden smiled with joy and hugged her dad. Then she turned to

Gabrielle, who'd obviously managed to successfully drive Grandpa Charles to his granddaughter's wedding.

"Thank you," she said sincerely.

"You're welcome," said Gabrielle.

Mrs. Camden felt tears welling up in her eyes. *So much for Gabrielle being a bad omen,* she thought.

As the small wedding party assembled at the back of the church, Ben Kinkirk greeted Mary Camden. It was the first time they'd seen each other since their breakup.

"You could have called," Mary told Ben as she took his arm.

"You could have called," Ben countered.

"Maybe I did," said Mary.

"Did you?" Ben said, surprised.

"No," Mary replied.

The music swelled and the wedding procession began. First came Lucy's twin brothers, walking side by side down the aisle, balancing their ring bearers' white silk pillows in their small hands. Next came Ruthie in her pastel gown and high heels, holding a bouquet of flowers.

Finally came Mary in her flight attendant's outfit, escorted by Ben in his still rumpled traveling clothes.

"I came to Florida," Ben whispered to Mary as they slowly moved along with the organ music, forced smiles plastered to their faces. "I tried to find you."

It was Mary's turn to be surprised. "When?"

Ben knew he'd zinged her. "Last week," he said with a smirk.

"I was in Buffalo."

With all eyes in the church on them, they gritted their teeth and continued walking.

"So," Ben said. "Are you seeing anyone?"

"Maybe," Mary shot back. "Are you seeing anyone?"

"Maybe," said Ben. "Hey, wait a minute. Have you seen Robbie since he moved to Florida?"

Mary didn't think this was a very good moment for Ben to be grilling her about her old boyfriend, but she didn't have time to reply anyway. They'd reached the end of the aisle, and it was time for them to part.

Mary moved left to stand beside Ruthie, and Ben moved right to take his place beside Kevin and Simon.

Still gritting his teeth, Ben stared at Mary. Today might be the happiest day of his brother's life, thought Ben, but, so far, it wasn't much fun for him. He wanted some answers from his old girlfriend. And before this day was over, he intended to get them.

A moment later, the congregation rose. In her white bridal gown and veil, a beaming Lucy was just starting to make her way to the front of the church, escorted by her older brother, Matt.

Looking toward the altar, Lucy could see her bridegroom waiting for her—right beside her father. The wedding of Kevin Kinkirk and Lucy Camden was finally about to begin.

# ELEVEN

"This is working out perfectly!" Lucy told her mother. "The wedding album is half filled, and we still have about half the pictures to look through."

"The photos taken in the church are just lovely. You looked beautiful, and Kevin looked so handsome," Mrs. Camden said. "Your dad looked pretty handsome, too."

Embarrassed, Reverend Camden changed the subject. "Once we actually started the ceremony, the service went pretty well, right?"

Lucy nodded. "The service was perfect, Dad. You were perfect. And the decorations. The organist, the congregation . . . everything and everyone was perfect."

"Except you flubbed your line," said Ruthie. "Dad said, 'Do you, Lucy . . .' And you jumped in with 'I do' before he could finish the question."

Ruthie raised an eyebrow at Lucy. "You only had one line. You might have rehearsed it."

"I said 'I do' so fast because at that point I knew that I really, really did," said Lucy.

"Well, I still say I'm not getting married until I'm thirty," Ruthie declared. "Even if Peter asks me tomorrow."

"Let's hope that doesn't happen," Mrs. Camden said. "We've had enough weddings in this family—for the next few months, at least."

Ruthie frowned. "I told you, I'm going to elope, and I mean it."

"Don't you want a nice wedding in your father's church?" Mrs. Camden asked.

"I wouldn't mind the wedding, but I'd rather have my reception at Ocean World Sea Life Park than in our church basement," said Ruthie. "At least at Ocean World we'd have a few dolphins to go with all the water!"

The living room was quiet for a

moment, and then Lucy burst out laughing. Reverend Camden looked at his daughter, surprised but happy she could laugh about it all now. Then he began to laugh, too.

Soon everyone was laughing. They all remembered what had happened right after the wedding service had ended. And they all had to admit that Ruthie was right: Ocean World was a pretty good description. . . .

With the joyous recessional music playing, the bride and groom walked down the center aisle together. At the back of the church, guests gathered to congratulate the couple.

Kevin shook many hands, and Lucy received kisses from friends, church members, and her entire family.

"Perhaps we should move downstairs for the reception," Simon announced in a loud voice, determined to perform his best-man duties smoothly and efficiently.

"Shall we go, Mrs. Kinkirk?" Kevin asked Lucy.

"Certainly, Mr. Kinkirk," Lucy replied with a giggle.

With that, Lucy's new husband took her

arm and led her through the room. Lucy and Kevin descended the stairs to the Glenoak Community Church special events space, a large room in the basement.

At the bottom of the stairs, Lucy distinctly heard the sound of tinkling water.

*Could it be?* she wondered excitedly.

While preparing for the wedding, Lucy and Mrs. Camden met with a caterer who had offered to rent them a large working fountain as the centerpiece for their reception. Lucy thought it was a lovely idea, but the price was way too high.

Now she wondered if her family had splurged and rented the fountain after all—until she saw the look of despair on her mother's face.

Ruthie rushed up to Lucy and Kevin. "You don't want to go in there."

Kevin gave Ruthie a look, then turned to Lucy. His bride's forehead was wrinkled with worry. Kevin placed his hands on her shoulders.

"Wait here," he said.

Then Kevin stepped up to the double doors and pushed them open. Over her groom's tuxedo-clad shoulder, Lucy saw tables with white tablecloths, lots and lots of beautiful flowers, and a huge pile of gifts. She also heard the distinctive sound of running water—louder now, almost like a waterfall!

Suddenly water gushed out of the room and into the hallway. Kevin, Simon, and a few of the guests close to the door jumped backward to avoid the tide.

Kevin shut the doors again, but not before Mario Vitale—owner of Bravo, Mario's Restaurant and the caterer for Lucy's reception—came running through them. The little bald man was wearing a tuxedo that was, from the knees down, soaking wet.

He turned and opened the double doors a crack.

"Move everything, pronto!" he cried to the catering staff, who were hurrying around the flooded special events room. His admonishment was followed by a string of words in Italian.

Then he saw Kevin.

"Oh, Mr. Kinkirk," he said. "Not to worry. Mr. Carter, one of the guests—"

"Bill Carter, of Carter Brothers Roofing?" Reverend Camden asked, appearing at Kevin's side.

Mr. Vitale nodded. "He said one of your drainpipes on the roof was probably blocked. . . . That rainwater from the storm gathered up there, then came down through the walls to the basement."

"You mean—"

"You're flooded, Reverend," said Bill Carter, emerging from the events space in his best suit, now soaked through. "I did my best to stop the water. I opened the drain in the floor. . . . You should be emptied out in a few hours. Have to cancel the reception, though."

"Oh, no!" Lucy cried.

"That will not happen!" Mr. Vitale promised. "My restaurant is only a few blocks away. The storm has chased away my customers, so we'll move Lucy and Kevin's reception there."

"Thank you, Mr. Vitale," said Kevin, shaking the little man's hand.

"Oh, Mr. Vitale," Mrs. Camden cried, hugging him. "How can we ever repay you?"

Mr. Vitale put up his hands. "Never worry about that—you and the reverend have done so much for the community already."

Then Mr. Vitale yelled some more

orders in Italian to his staff inside the events room.

"Let my people get the stuff into the van. We'll be set up at Bravo, Mario's in half an hour."

Kevin hurried to Lucy's side.

"I'm sorry about all this," he said.

But Lucy just shook her head. "Don't worry," she told him. "It's not your fault. And anyway, we got married. That's the important thing. Whatever else that goes wrong won't change that."

Kevin smiled and kissed her.

"I love you, Mrs. Lucy Kinkirk."

Lucy felt a thrill run through her every time Kevin said her brand-new name.

*That's me! I'm Mrs. Lucy Kinkirk!*

Lucy and Kevin went back upstairs while the caterers moved all the food and tableware into a van that would take it back to the restaurant. At the same time, Matt, Mary, Simon, Ruthie, and even Reverend and Mrs. Camden loaded up every car they could—even Kevin's—with the wedding decorations and presents and drove everything to Bravo, Mario's.

Lucy and Kevin stayed at the church and continued to greet their wedding

guests and pose for photos at the altar.
After about forty-five minutes, Lucy
tapped Kevin.

"I think we should go to the restaurant,"
she said. "Everything's probably ready now."

As if on cue, the doors to the church
opened and Simon and Ben Kinkirk
appeared.

"Your car awaits," Ben announced.

"Car?" asked Lucy. "I thought the
restaurant was close enough to walk."

"No way," said Simon. "It's still raining, so Ben and I, as your joint best men,
figured it was our duty to get you there in
style." He opened a large black umbrella
and handed it to Kevin.

Dodging the raindrops from the storm
that still stubbornly hung over Glenoak,
Kevin and Lucy huddled close beneath the
umbrella and followed Ben and Simon.
Concerned with staying dry, the couple
barely saw the vehicle until they reached
the large black car door, which Simon
opened with a bow.

"Wow," said Kevin as he helped Lucy
into the backseat. "How the heck did you
rent a limo so fast?"

Ben Kinkirk smiled. "Nothing's too

good for my brother and brand-new sister-in-law!"

Kevin—always suspicious of his brother—turned around and looked at the back of the limo, behind the plush seats. His eyes went wide. Lucy tried to follow his gaze, but Kevin turned her head with a kiss.

"What was that for?" Lucy asked.

"That's because I love you," Kevin replied.

Ben grinned in the rearview mirror. "Kevin just doesn't want you to know where your limo came from."

"What's the difference where it came from?" Lucy asked.

"That's the spirit, Luce," said Simon from the passenger seat. "After all, you didn't expect to have to move your reception, did you? But you did. So Ben and I decided flexibility was the theme for the day."

They pulled the car right up to the front door of Bravo, Mario's. A parking attendant opened the door.

If the attendant was surprised to see a bride and groom emerge from this particular car, he didn't show it.

"They're here!" Ruthie cried from inside the door.

Mrs. Camden hurried to greet Lucy. "Come inside," she said. "The restaurant really looks great. Mr. Vitale set up the main dining room with lights and everything!"

As soon as Lucy and Kevin were out of the car, Ben pulled away. Unfortunately, the tires squealed on the wet pavement, causing Lucy to turn her head.

As Ben drove around the corner, Lucy could read the inscription painted on the rear doors of the limousine quite clearly: BENJAMIN FIDDLE & SONS FUNERAL HOME AND MORTUARY.

The car wasn't a limousine at all—it was a hearse!

Kevin saw the stunned look cross Lucy's face. He took her hand and squeezed it.

"Forget about that," he said. "We're together. We're finally here at the reception. Nothing else can go wrong."

Lucy smiled, but she didn't believe him. In fact, she got the feeling this night of weird surprises was only beginning.

# TWELVE

"Close your eyes!" Mrs. Camden said as she took hold of Lucy's right hand. Kevin held her left.

"Now keep them closed. We'll lead the way." Mrs. Camden guided her daughter to the center of the dining room.

All around, Lucy could hear the excited voices of the reception guests. Her eyes remained dutifully shut.

"Take a step down," said Kevin. Lucy lowered her toe until she felt the floor under her high-heeled shoe.

"Now just five more steps," Mrs. Camden said. Lucy really wanted to open her eyes, but she resisted the temptation. As a rule, surprises were as important to the surpriser as to the surprisee—and Lucy didn't want to spoil anybody's fun.

"All ready?" Mrs. Camden asked.

Lucy nodded.

"Open your eyes!" Mrs. Camden cried.

She did.

Lucy gasped when she saw the interior of the restaurant. In a little less than an hour, Mr. Vitale, his staff, and the members of the wedding party had transformed a simple restaurant dining room into a fairyland of tiny festive lights, silk-draped table settings, and sweet-smelling flowers.

"Oh, it's lovely!" Lucy cried.

Mr. Vitale stood nearby, puffed up with pride. Next to him, his wife, Maria, began to clap for the bride and groom. Everyone in the room joined in. Lucy curtsied and Kevin bowed.

"Thank you," said Lucy. "Thank you all so much for coming here tonight . . . for being a part of this special evening."

"Let me escort you to your table," said Simon, appearing at their side.

Flashbulbs popped and video cameras rolled as Simon led Lucy and Kevin through the throng of guests to a table for two at the front of the room.

Sitting on a white silk-draped table, a lovely bouquet of red roses set off two gorgeous settings of crystal, silver, and fine china. Next to the bride and groom's table stood a wonderfully decorated four-tiered wedding cake that Lucy thought was almost too beautiful to eat.

When the bride and groom arrived at their table, Lucy turned to her husband. "This is the most wonderful day of my life."

Everyone stood, still clapping, still cheering. Filled with joy, Lucy took in the scene, her eyes welling with tears as she tried to burn this moment into her memory forever—the faces of her brothers and sisters, her mother and father, and her husband.

Then Lucy's gaze landed on the Colonel's housekeeper, Gabrielle. The woman met her eyes and smiled warmly.

"And I thought she was a bad omen," Lucy murmured to herself. "How could I have been so silly?"

But as Lucy's eyes took in the room's lights and flowers and lovely decorations, a flash of lightning zigzagged across the night sky outside the restaurant's tall, rain-streaked windows. A split second later there was a pulsing rumble, followed by an earsplitting peal of thunder that shook the entire restaurant!

All of the lights in the building—and out on the street, too—winked once and went out.

Inside the dining room, total darkness descended. For a moment, there was dead silence, too. Then Lucy heard cries of alarm. One woman screamed. A moment later the battery-powered emergency lights came on, dully illuminating the exit signs with an eerie, scarlet glow.

"Power's out," a voice called.

"Duh!" someone replied.

"What do we do now?" asked someone else.

Another flash of lightning and peal of thunder followed. Across the street, a small branch split off from a tree and fell on some parked cars.

A man yelled, "That's my SUV!"

A woman gasped in shock.

Then the room exploded with a babel

of voices, none of which Kevin or Lucy could understand.

"Calm down, everyone!" Kevin suddenly bellowed in his most commanding policeman's tone.

"Quiet down now!" Roxanne yelled, determined to offer her partner backup, even at his own wedding reception.

The room slowly quieted down.

"There's no reason to panic," Kevin announced. "We're here to celebrate a wedding and that's what we're going to do—lights or no lights."

Just then Lucy noticed a flickering flame floating in the darkness beyond the dining room. A moment later Mr. Vitale emerged from the gloom, a lit candle in his hand.

"Don't worry," the man said. "The gas is still working, so the food will be hot and plentiful. We've got plenty of ice for drinks. And lots of candles, too. Let the celebration begin!"

Some people applauded. Others seemed doubtful.

Kevin turned to Lucy. "What do you say, Luce?" he asked.

Lucy didn't even have to ponder her reply. She smiled so brightly, it practically lit up the darkened room.

Turning, Lucy reached out and took the candle from Mr. Vitale's hand. Bending low, she touched the flame to the candle on her table until it, too, began to burn.

Then she stood up again and faced the audience, her face illuminated by the flickering flame.

"I say it's better to light a candle than to curse the darkness," she said, loud enough for everyone to hear her.

Lucy's wise words were greeted by laughter and applause.

With Kevin's hand in hers, Lucy went to each table and touched her candle to the wick of all the others. At each stop, the guests gave Kevin a hug and kissed Lucy's cheek.

But not everyone was in such a festive mood. Ever since their walk down the aisle, Mary had been actively dodging Ben Kinkirk. As Kevin and Lucy circled the room, Ben finally managed to corner Mary near the stack of wedding gifts.

Almost immediately, he began to interrogate her about her life in Florida and, more important, about who Mary was or was not dating.

"That's really none of your business," Mary replied. "Let it go."

A waiter stopped near them with a lit candle. In the glowing light, Mary got her first good look at Ben's face.

"Who gave you the shiner?" Mary asked, pointing to the now-darkening bruise under Ben's left eye.

"I ran into a door," said Ben.

"No, you didn't," said Mary, leaning closer. "You got in a fight."

"Just drop it, okay?"

Mary's eyebrow lifted. "Ben got in a fi-ight," she sang. "Ben got in a fi-ight."

"Cut it out!" said Ben. He tried to sound cool and casual, but deep down, his mood was growing more foul by the minute. This wasn't how his reunion with Mary Camden was supposed to go.

"Come on, who beat you up?" Mary asked.

"I'll have you know I won," said Ben, thrusting his thumb into his chest.

"So you admit it!" Mary cried triumphantly. "You did get in a fight! . . . But who with?"

Ben shook his head.

"Come on, tell me."

"That Hampton guy," Ben blurted. "Chandler what's his face."

Mary's eyes went wide. "Are you telling me that big, strong Ben Kinkirk, the rough, tough fireman, got a black eye from my father's gentle assistant minister?" Mary started to laugh.

"So he got in a few lucky hits. I told you I won!" Ben insisted, getting angrier.

"Funny," Mary said with glee. "You don't look like you won. In fact, you're beginning to swell up. Are you sure you didn't get hit by a truck instead of the gentle Reverend Hampton?"

Ben was really steamed now. Worse, he was actually feeling embarrassed. And in front of Mary Camden!

It was probably the worst possible moment for Ben to spot Chandler Hampton on the other side of the room. Of course, that was exactly what happened.

"I'll show you who beat up who!" Ben warned.

"Uh-oh," said Mary, realizing what she'd started. She quickly reached out to stop Ben.

Too late. Ben turned on his heel and started across the room, aiming for Chandler Hampton. The young minister had his back turned to Ben.

Mary looked around for help. Her eyes met Matt's and she silently motioned toward Ben.

Matt had been standing nearby and heard the entire conversation. And he saved the day—well, almost saved the day.

As Ben charged across the crowded room, Matt stuck his foot out to trip him.

That move stopped a potential fight. Unfortunately, when Ben fell, he slid across the pastry table. There was a collective gasp of horror as he plunged headlong—with a resounding splat—right into Lucy and Kevin's beautiful four-tiered wedding cake!

"I can't believe Sam Fuller got a picture of that moment!" Reverend Camden said, holding up the photo.

"I can't believe it happened," said Mrs. Camden with a sigh.

"Good thing he only messed up half the cake," said Simon.

"And Mr. Vitale's pastry chef could still serve the rest for dessert," added Ruthie.

Lucy took the photo and studied it.

"If I had known Kevin's family was so crazy, I might have had second thoughts about marrying him."

"Honey," Mrs. Camden said, patting Lucy's hand. "You did have second thoughts. Remember?"

"Okay, third thoughts, then," said Lucy.

"How do you think Mary felt?" Ruthie asked. "Ben Kinkirk is only your brother-in-law. But Mary actually dated that lunkhead!"

"He's not really so bad," said Simon. "And Mary did egg him on."

"True," said Lucy. "Mary felt so bad, she actually ended up dancing with Ben most of the night. Although I suspect she was just doing it to make sure he stayed out of trouble."

"And out of Reverend Hampton's way," added Ruthie.

Simon picked up a picture that showed the guests going crazy on the restaurant's makeshift dance floor. "Whoa, we really rocked the house that night, didn't we?" said Simon.

"If you exclude doing the hokey pokey and the chicken dance," said Ruthie, "then, yeah, I guess we rocked the house."

# THIRTEEN

Her face flushed, Lucy collapsed into her chair and took a big gulp of icy water. Fanning herself with a napkin, she watched the wedding guests jumping to the pulsing music.

The lack of electricity had inspired one of the guests to retrieve a battery-powered boom box and a collection of CDs from the trunk of his car. Now most of the folks were up on their feet, dancing by candlelight.

Kevin appeared at Lucy's side. "Our flight out of here is going to take off without us if we don't make our escape pretty soon," he warned, tapping his wristwatch.

"Do you think the plane will actually fly in this weather?" asked Lucy.

"I had our best man phone the airline. Once the thunderstorm passed, Glenoak Airport started to let planes take off. I wouldn't be surprised if we were delayed, but right now our flight schedule is as planned."

Lucy grinned. "'As planned,' huh? Given that very little has gone off 'as planned' in the last forty-eight hours, I'd say that's a good omen."

"Let's get going," said Kevin.

Lucy was about to go change out of her dress when she heard someone on the dance floor yell, "Where are the bride and groom? Get them out here!"

"Oh, no," said Kevin, "they're forming a conga line."

"And they're headed our way," said Lucy.

Unable to escape the snaking dancers, Kevin and Lucy were scooped into their midst and carried back onto the dance floor.

On the other side of the dining room, calculating eyes watched the newlyweds' every move, waiting for a chance to pounce.

"Hey, sweetheart," Peter Petrowski called. "Who are you watching?"

Ruthie's eyes never left her prey as Peter crossed the room to get to her.

"Kevin and Lucy," Ruthie replied. "My timing has got to be perfect to pull this one off."

"This one?" said Peter, scratching his head. "This one what? Hey, wait a minute. Does this have anything to do with that package you want me to get from the car?"

Ruthie nodded. "You better be ready to move as soon as I give the signal, too. Timing is going to be crucial. And I may need you for a decoy. Stay alert."

"Are you sure you can't take more than water and tea?" Chandler Hampton asked, pushing a plate in his date's direction.

Roxanne shook her head and shoved the food away. Instead, she took a tiny sip from the cup on the table in front of her. "I'm lucky to keep this down," she said.

They were alone together at a quiet

table far from the dance floor. Chandler gently touched Roxanne's forehead. She still felt hot.

"I can take you home," Chandler suggested.

"No!" Roxanne cried. "If I leave before the bride and groom, they will never forgive me—especially Lucy."

"What's the problem between you two?"

"No problem, really," Roxanne replied. "It's just that I'm Kevin's partner, and police partners have a unique relationship. Law enforcement work can be pretty intense, and partners have to be able to trust each other with their lives. In the past, Lucy's felt threatened by that. She seems to be over it now, but I don't want to give her any reason to doubt my loyalty to both of them—and my respect for their wedding vows."

"Very commendable," Chandler observed.

Then he thought about it for a moment. "Maybe this partner thing is something I should worry about."

Roxanne leaned close and gave him a kiss on the cheek. "You never have to be jealous of anyone, Chandler."

Reverend Hampton blushed. "Why don't you try the cake?" he asked, changing the subject.

"Ugh!" Roxanne said, throwing up her hands. "I'm afraid I'd get a piece that had Ben Kinkirk's big fat head stuck in it."

Then Roxanne spied a shimmering white gown in the darkness.

"I'll be right back," she told Chandler, squeezing his hand.

She rose and caught up to Lucy. "Hey, Lucy, I—"

"Thank goodness it's you, Roxanne!" Lucy whispered, pulling her into the shadows.

"Kevin and I want to say our good-byes, but it's pretty hard with all the guests wanting to hug us and toast us and dance with us. We don't want to be rude, but we're going to miss our flight if we don't get going—"

"Say no more," Roxanne told her. "I'll be glad to help any way I can."

"Thanks!" said Lucy. "Would you mind grabbing my overnight bag from the front seat of Kevin's car, then meeting me in the ladies' room?"

"No problem," said Roxanne.

Lucy thrust a set of keys into Roxanne's palm and hurried away.

Roxanne dodged the rain in the parking lot as she retrieved the suitcase, then returned to the restaurant. Inside the door, she shook the rain from her jacket.

"Hi," said Ruthie. "What's up?"

Roxanne shushed her. "I'm getting your sister her overnight bag so that she and Kevin can get out of here. Don't tell anyone for now, okay? She needs some privacy to change out of her gown."

Ruthie gave Roxanne a thumbs-up. "You can count on me!"

As Roxanne headed for the ladies' room, Ruthie caught up with Peter at the buffet table.

"The word is given," Ruthie announced.

Peter immediately set down his plate and hurried out to the parking lot to fetch Ruthie's mysterious package.

Just that little bit of running to and from the car had made Roxanne weak and dizzy. It also made the tea she'd drunk a short time ago begin to churn in her stomach. By the time she reached the bathroom, Roxanne wasn't feeling very well at all.

Stumbling through the door, she found Lucy waiting for her.

"Did anyone see you?" Lucy asked.

"Just Ruthie," Roxanne said, holding her forehead. "I swore her to secrecy."

Lucy opened her bag and pulled out a blouse and a pair of jeans. She had bought a lovely cream-colored travel suit to wear on the plane, but she didn't want to ruin it in this weather. Lucy went into a stall and closed the door behind her.

"Guard the door, and don't let anyone in," she told Roxanne.

Pale and sweating now, Roxanne stumbled over to the door and leaned against it.

"What a day!" Lucy gushed. "I can't believe it's over. . . ."

"Uh-huh," Roxanne replied, rubbing her eyes.

There was a rustle of silk inside the stall. Then the door opened a crack.

"Roxanne, could you help me with this zipper?" Lucy asked. "I can't seem to get it down."

Roxanne slowly crossed the room. She grasped the handle and pulled on the zipper several times. Nothing happened.

"I think some material is caught between the teeth," Roxanne said.

While Roxanne fumbled with the zipper, Lucy talked.

"I thought the reception went fine, considering there was no electricity," she said. "Everyone seemed to enjoy the food, but I was too nervous to eat. How was it? The fish smelled good, and the lasagna looked tasty, too."

The food talk got Roxanne's stomach churning again. She released the zipper and put her hands to her mouth.

"Are you okay?" Lucy asked.

"I'm . . . gonna . . . hurl!"

Roxanne pushed Lucy out of the stall and slammed the door behind her. Then she started to throw up.

"Oh . . . oh, no . . . oh, no," Lucy cried. "What do I do?"

"Don't . . . do . . . anything . . . ," Roxanne gasped.

But Lucy ignored her. "I'll get help!" she cried.

Lucy burst through the door to the women's room. In the hallway near the pay phones, she found Mrs. Vitale.

"I need help!" Lucy cried. "Someone is very sick in the ladies' room."

"Oh, dear!" Maria Vitale said. "Was it the food, maybe?"

"Well, we were talking about the food, but I don't know what she ate exactly."

"This is terrible!" Mrs. Vitale cried. "We've never had food poisoning! Never before in this restaurant."

Lucy tried to calm the woman, but Mrs. Vitale started yelling in Italian for someone named Anthony. Two waiters and a man wearing a chef's hat appeared a moment later.

"I knew you'd be trouble. I told my husband to hire my cousin, but no, he hired you instead. And now look what you've done. You've poisoned a guest!" Mrs. Vitale yelled, shaking her finger at the chef.

"That is not possible!" the chef cried. "I have eaten the food myself. It is *bellissimo*!"

"If it's so good, how did this happen?" Mrs. Vitale cried, throwing open the ladies' room door. Inside, Roxanne made sick noises that echoed off the tile walls.

"She's sick because of you!" Mrs. Vitale shouted. "This could ruin us. Bravo, Mario's will have to close its doors from all the lawsuits!"

Then the chef launched into a string of Italian words, all of them sounding angry. Mr. Vitale showed up, and the shouting got louder—in both Italian and English. Finally the chef tore off his hat, threw it on the floor, and stomped on it. Then he turned on his heel and walked away, cursing loudly. The waiters chased after him.

Meanwhile, a crowd had started to gather. Some of the wedding guests heard the words *sick* and *poisoned* and started to worry. Rumors quickly spread throughout the dining room.

Lucy stood helplessly by, trying to quell the panic, stop the argument, and get Roxanne some medical attention.

Dr. Hastings and his wife pushed through the crowd. "What's going on, Lucy?" the doctor demanded.

"Come with me," Lucy cried, grabbing her uncle's hand and dragging him into the bathroom.

\* \* \*

A series of beeps sounded as the digital thermometer finished taking Roxanne's temperature. Dr. Hastings took the device out of the sick woman's mouth and studied the tiny numbers on the display.

"You have a fever," he announced loud enough for all of the guests to hear. "And you're obviously nauseated. You also complain about pain in your joints, correct?"

Roxanne nodded.

"And when did these symptoms begin?"

"Last night," said Roxanne. "Or early this morning, depending on how you look at it."

Dr. Hastings turned and faced the crowd—which included Mr. and Mrs. Vitale and Anthony the chef, who had to be convinced to return.

"This young lady has the flu, that's all," he declared. "There is no food poisoning involved. Mr. Vitale's food is nothing but delicious and expertly prepared."

There was a collective sigh of relief. Chandler draped his jacket over Roxanne's shoulders and she pulled it around her.

After a few minutes the crowd thinned

until only Lucy, Kevin, Dr. Hastings, Chandler, and Roxanne remained.

"Now I want Chandler here to take you home immediately," Dr. Hastings told Roxanne, "where you are to go to bed and sleep for as long as you can."

Then Dr. Hastings reached into the medical bag he'd retrieved from his car. "Take these." He thrust some pills into her hand. "Drink plenty of fluids, and if the symptoms persist, call me in the morning."

"Thanks, Dr. Hastings," Chandler said, extending his hand.

But Roxanne slapped it away. "Don't thank that . . . that . . . that plague carrier! I wouldn't be sick if it wasn't for him. And I wouldn't be surprised if he charged me for his treatment. Heck of a way to drum up business! I ought to—"

Suddenly Roxanne clutched her stomach. Then she shot to her feet and raced to the women's room. Sick sounds emerged a moment later.

Dr. Hastings shook his head. "She can't possibly have caught the flu from me. I already had it two weeks ago, and I'm no longer contagious."

"I know," Chandler said, shaking Hank's hand. "And when she's more rational and more rested, I expect she'll realize that."

"Good," said Dr. Hastings. "Now if you don't mind, I'm going to get back to my wife."

"Lucy!" a voice called a moment later.

Lucy turned to see her mother and Mrs. Vitale standing near a door with big letters that read EMPLOYEES ONLY.

"We have a place where you can change your clothes in peace," Mrs. Camden said. "Then we'll see that you and Kevin make it out of here so you can catch your plane."

# FOURTEEN

Kevin knocked on the door marked EMPLOYEES ONLY. It opened a crack and Lucy peeked out.

"All clear," Kevin whispered.

Lucy opened the door wide and stepped into the hallway. She was dressed in a new pink tank top, rain jacket, jeans, and sneakers. Mrs. Camden followed her, a garment bag containing Lucy's wedding gown draped over her arm.

"Straight through here to the door," Simon said, motioning the newlyweds on a route that took them through the restaurant's kitchen. "You're running too late to make a formal exit now.

"Good luck and God bless you both,"

said Simon as they hurried through the kitchen doors.

In the kitchen itself they found Mary and Matt waiting for them at a row of stainless steel refrigerators. They both gave Lucy a big hug and shook Kevin's hand.

"Have a great time," Matt said.

At the opposite end of the kitchen, another door opened and Reverend Camden gave them a thumbs-up.

"I want to thank you for letting me join your family," Kevin said, shaking the reverend's hand.

"It's our honor, really," said Reverend Camden. "You're a good man. Lucy was lucky to find you. . . . Now go!"

"Bye, Dad," Lucy said. Giving her father a final hug, she felt tears well up in her eyes. Then Lucy hugged her mother and the tears ran down her cheeks.

"I'll give everyone your thanks," said Mrs. Camden, her own cheeks wet. "Now hurry, before you miss your plane."

Kevin's car was waiting for them at the front entrance. He unlocked the trunk and dumped Lucy's overnight bag with the rest of their luggage. It was still raining, and thunder began to rumble again in the night sky. The roads were dark and slick.

"One more thing before I go," Kevin said.

"Hurry!" Lucy exclaimed. "We're going to be late."

Kevin circled his car once, then twice. When he came around the second time, Lucy rolled down her window.

"What are you doing? A flight check?"

"I just wanted to make sure there are no signs or cans or streamers on my car," Kevin replied.

Lucy nodded her understanding.

Earlier that week, Kevin gave Ruthie and Simon a lecture when they hinted they were going to cover his car with streamers and washable paint that said JUST MARRIED.

Kevin told them in no uncertain terms that he wanted no signs, balloons, streamers, tin cans, old shoes, or anything else tied to his car.

Lucy chuckled at the memory. Ever the cop, her new husband had warned them that newlywed signs on cars were a distraction and therefore a traffic hazard.

"All clear?" Lucy asked.

"All clear," said Kevin.

Just then, someone called his name. Kevin turned to see Peter Petrowski, Ruthie's friend, hurrying up to him.

"What's wrong?" asked Kevin.

"Nothing's wrong," Peter replied. "It's just that . . . Well, I wanted to say congratulations!"

Peter thrust out his hand and Kevin, puzzled, shook it.

"You're a real role model for me," Peter continued. "And I wanted to give you and Mrs. Kinkirk my best wishes. . . ."

While Peter distracted Kevin, Ruthie darted from the shadows and ducked behind Kevin's car.

Using two wires she had wrapped around her wrist, Ruthie strapped a large, rectangular, plastic-covered parcel on Kevin's rear bumper.

When she was sure it was secure, Ruthie yanked off the protective plastic wrapping and ran back to her hiding place.

". . . So have a great time, Officer Kinkirk," Peter said when he spied Ruthie making her getaway. The boy waved one more time and hurried off.

"What do you know?" said Kevin, grinning from ear to ear. "Looks like I'm a role model to Ruthie's little friend."

With that, Kevin started the engine and pulled out of the parking lot. Plainly visible to anyone driving behind his car was a hand-painted sign affixed to the bumper.

In big, waterproof, glow-in-the-dark letters it read HONK FOR THE NEWLYWEDS.

As they merged onto the highway, Kevin let out a big sigh of relief.

"Thank goodness it's over," he said. "Now we don't have to be the center of attention anymore tonight."

Lucy sat back and smiled, remembering the day. Her musings were interrupted by the car behind them. The driver kept beeping his horn.

"Go on, pass me if you're in such a hurry," said Kevin to the other driver, motioning him forward.

But the car just stayed on their tail, honking continuously, until it pulled off at the next exit. A car full of teenage girls honked at them, too.

"What is all this honking about?" Kevin cried. "If I were on duty, I'd cite them for disturbing the peace."

The honking continued for quite some time, and Kevin remained totally puzzled. Finally they rounded the turn that marked the final stretch to the airport.

Kevin noticed the traffic ahead of them had begun to slow considerably. He peered through the intermittent swipes of the windshield wipers, trying to determine the cause of the delay.

"Looks like an accident," he said. "Everything is at a standstill ahead of us."

"Are we going to make it to the airport?" Lucy asked.

"The airport's at the next exit," he told her. "Only a mile from here."

"So you're saying we'll make it?"

Kevin smiled at his new wife. "We'll make it."

Just then, the car in front of them came to a complete stop. As Kevin slowed, the car directly behind his honked once, twice, three times. Kevin stared into the rearview mirror.

"I'm stuck same as you, pal! I can't go anywhere, so it's no use honking!"

The other lane of traffic slowed but continued to move. As an SUV passed their car, it honked, loud and long enough to make Kevin jump.

"What the—?"

The car behind the SUV honked as it passed them, too. The driver and his passenger even waved. Then a truck went slowly by, the horn shattering their ears.

Finally, on the right shoulder of the road, a motorcycle streaked past Kevin's car. That driver honked, too, and waved as he went by. Kevin could see the cyclist grinning under his safety helmet.

"Why is everybody honking at me?" yelled Kevin. "I'm a good driver! I'm not doing anything wrong. It's just that the traffic isn't moving! If it isn't moving in front of me, how can I go anywhere?"

Kevin was definitely losing it. Lucy gently touched his shoulder. "Calm down, sweetheart."

"Sorry," Kevin said. "It's just—"

He was interrupted by another honking horn.

"That's it!" Kevin cried. He turned in time to see a Glenoak police car pull up along the shoulder of the road and roll to a halt right behind his car. To Kevin's surprise, Sergeant Saunders, one of his superiors, emerged from the vehicle.

The man checked Kevin's rear bumper, then shook his head. He pulled the ticket book out of his pocket and walked to Kevin's window.

"Sarge," Kevin said as he rolled down his window. "I'm so glad to see you. My bride and I are trying to get to the airport up ahead and—"

"License and registration, please," said Sergeant Saunders, his voice businesslike.

Kevin blinked in surprise. "Sarge, it's me!"

"License and registration, please," Saunders repeated, shining a flashlight into Kevin's face.

Kevin slapped his hands on the steering wheel. Then, surrendering, he reached into his pocket and pulled out his wallet. He tore the license out of its pocket and handed it to Sergeant Saunders.

The policeman studied the license, then shone a light into Kevin's face to compare the driver's license photo with the actual driver.

"Are you aware that it is illegal to have a

sign on your bumper?" Sergeant Saunders said, handing the license back to Kevin.

"Huh?" said Kevin.

"Signs are illegal unless they are painted on the vehicle," Saunders said, a smile beginning to crack through his stern visage.

Kevin looked at Lucy. Lucy looked at Kevin.

"Ruthie!" they cried together.

Saunders laughed and walked to the rear bumper. He returned a moment later, the offending sign in hand.

"Congratulations, Kevin," Sergeant Saunders said, shaking his hand through the open window. "Wish I could have come to the wedding, but somebody's got to be on duty on a night like this."

Kevin took the sign and tossed it in the backseat.

"Funny joke, Sarge," Kevin said sheepishly. "Pulling me over, I mean."

"I just thought with a jackknifed trailer blocking part of the road ahead of you, you two lovebirds might need a police escort to the airport."

Lucy clapped with glee.

"Lead on, Sergeant," Kevin said.

Minutes later, with sirens blaring and lights flashing, Sergeant Saunders raced along the shoulder of the road. Kevin Kinkirk followed closely behind.

"That sign was a dirty trick," Lucy told Ruthie as she gazed at a picture of their car pulling out of Bravo, Mario's parking lot. "Why did you do that after Kevin asked you not to?"

"I took it as a challenge," Ruthie replied with a shrug. "Kevin should know that telling me not to do something is like throwing down a glove in a duel. Sooner or later I'm going to do it."

"So, Lucy, what did Kevin actually say to Ruthie when you two got back from your honeymoon?" asked Simon.

"I don't know," said Lucy. "Kevin just told me it was between him and Ruthie."

Simon turned to Ruthie. "He must have really given it to you."

"Actually he didn't," admitted Ruthie. "He just gave me the sign back and said in that scary cop voice he uses, 'Someday you're going to get married, and it will be my turn.'"

"Whoa!" Simon cried. "That's worse than getting yelled at."

Ruthie nodded. "Yet another good reason to elope."

"We've got about forty-five minutes," Kevin said, glancing at his watch as they passed through the glass doors of the airport. "I think we can still make it."

At the counter, an airline attendant took their tickets.

"Whew." Kevin sighed. "I'm going to sleep the whole flight."

"Good," said Lucy. "Because when we start our honeymoon, you won't have time to sleep. I plan on having fun every single second of our trip!"

"Excuse me, Mr. and Mrs. Kinkirk," the airline attendant said, interrupting them. "I regret to inform you that your flight has been canceled. In fact, all flights have been canceled due to the bad weather until further notice. . . ."

# FIFTEEN

"We could drive back to your parents' house," Kevin suggested to Lucy with a frown. Lucy knew that course of action wouldn't please him any more than it would her. She shook her head.

"Might I suggest the hotel on the other side of our parking lot?" the airline attendant said. "That way you won't have to travel far to get back to the airport, and we can try to find you a new flight in the morning."

"Thank you," Kevin said.

"Very much," Lucy added.

Unfortunately, they learned to their dismay that the Airport Inn was full.

In fact, the place was so crowded, there were even people sleeping in the lobby. Although the airport had been open for part of the day, the storms had backed up a huge number of flights. Hundreds of travelers had become stranded, and they had gobbled up all the available hotel rooms by now.

"You could try the Mohawk Express Motel at the corner of Clark Road and Ashton Street," the desk clerk suggested. "Or the Castle Lodge on Smith Highway. Here's the phone book if you want to look up their numbers."

Kevin tried to turn on his cell phone, only to realize that he had forgotten to charge it. It was dead. "Can you call ahead for us?" Kevin asked. "Those hotels are miles apart in the opposite direction, and it's getting on toward midnight."

"I would love to call, Mr. Kinkirk," the man replied with a frown. "But unfortunately our phones failed when a tree fell on some telephone wires."

Back in the car, it was a coin toss that made the decision. Soon the newlyweds were off on a long and harrowing drive to the Castle Lodge.

The short desk clerk with little round glasses was sympathetic but initially claimed he had no rooms. At that point, Kevin pulled the man aside while Lucy plopped herself down into a soft chair in the lobby.

"We've just been married," Kevin whispered to the clerk. "Our flight out of here was canceled, and we need a place to sleep for a few hours until morning. Can't you find something? We'll take anything."

The desk clerk thought about it for a long time. "Wait here," he said.

The clerk crossed the lobby and knocked on a door marked MANAGER before entering. Kevin heard voices, some of them loud, coming from behind the door.

At one point the door opened a crack and a harried-looking man with shaggy gray hair and bushy gray eyebrows peeked out. Kevin waved. The door quickly shut again.

Finally the desk clerk with the little round glasses emerged. He gestured, and a thin, bald bellhop in a dark blue uniform appeared at his side. The desk clerk called him Phillips.

"We have a linen station that can be made available as a room, so we've summoned the chambermaid to fix it up," the desk clerk explained. "When I heard you were newlyweds—well, I told the manager we simply had to do something!"

The desk clerk nodded to Phillips.

"Phillips will call you when the room is ready. So if you would kindly wait in the lobby. . . ."

Fifteen minutes later, Lucy was walking arm in arm with Kevin, her footsteps echoing along one of the hotel's empty corridors. Through absolute darkness, she and her husband followed the flickering candle flames that illuminated the passage. Apparently the electricity had gone out here as well.

Lucy glanced at her watch, its glow-in-the-dark face barely visible in the gloom. Midnight. The witching hour. With a shiver, Lucy gripped Kevin's arm tighter. He patted her hand reassuringly. It was a nice gesture, but it failed to reassure Lucy in the least.

She felt like she'd been suddenly thrown into some strange gothic nightmare. *Maybe*

*I'll wake up from this,* she thought. *And I'll find myself in a luxury hotel room in some faraway paradise with Kevin by my side.*

Unfortunately, there was no paradise ahead—only Phillips. The bald man's head, in the wavering candlelight, reminded Lucy of a pink skull.

Above his shoulder, the man held a silver candelabra. The strange morphing shadows cast from its sputtering flames seemed to crawl up the walls and along the ceiling.

"Most of our guests have retired for the evening," said Phillips. "You were indeed fortunate to get this suite. It is such a lovely space and, in fact, was originally a bridal suite. Such a shame our hotel manager has failed to use it that way for so long."

The man grinned, showing a row of sharp white teeth. "And now, finally, we have newlyweds to sleep in our bridal suite once again."

"Did I hear the desk clerk say the room was being used as a linen closet?" Kevin asked.

"More of a linen station, actually," Phillips corrected him. "But the Master—"

"The Master?" Lucy cried, thoughts of an evil count dancing in her head.

"The Masterpiece Hotel Corporation, our parent company. They've been pushing for our management to open this suite for commercial use. Ever since—"

Phillips suddenly stopped, sealing his thin lips, as if he'd almost revealed too much.

"Since?" Lucy asked.

After a long pause, Phillips replied, "Since Masterpiece Hotel Corporation purchased this hotel."

Why did Lucy think this man had meant to say something else entirely?

"Ah! Here we are at last," said Phillips.

The trio stood before a pair of double doors with large brass handles and carved wood cherubs and hearts. Appropriate symbols of this special night, perhaps, but to Lucy they looked somehow threatening in the eerie darkness.

"Lucky us," quipped Kevin.

"Indeed," sniffed Phillips.

Outside the window at the far end of the hallway, lightning ripped the night sky, followed by a rumble of thunder.

"Despite the loss of power, the chambermaid has tried to make the suite as comfortable as possible for you, our very special guests."

Phillips reached out and gripped the brass handles with both hands. He twisted them and pushed. The doors opened with a forlorn creak and he stepped aside.

Lucy held tight to her husband's arm as they walked past the man and into the room.

Though the Castle Lodge was an old hotel—with a turn-of-the-century-style lobby, wrought-iron elevators, and long marble hallways—those areas seemed almost ultramodern when compared to the cluttered Victorian decor of this old bridal suite.

Scarlet velvet curtains hung from the walls. The dressers and standing closets were made of dark heavy wood. A full-length mirror covered one wall, its gilt frame shining dully in the glow cast by a dozen candles on dressers and night tables.

A large four-poster bed with a heavy velvet canopy dominated the room. Lacy pillows were strewn about the bed and on stiff wooden chairs—they were even scattered across a large hardwood trunk that sat at the foot of the bed.

"Looks like something out of a movie," said Kevin.

"Yeah," Lucy replied. "A vampire movie!"

"This room's elegance speaks of a bygone era," said Phillips proudly.

"Whatever," Lucy replied.

"The maid will bring you some clean towels," Phillips said. "May I bring your luggage up from your vehicle?"

"I just need my overnight bag," said Lucy. "The rest can stay in the trunk."

"I'll go with you," Kevin told the man.

Lucy clutched his arm. "And leave me here alone?" she squeaked.

"Come on, Luce." Kevin chuckled. "It's just an empty room. Anyway, I'll be back before you notice I'm even gone."

After Kevin left, Lucy paced the room nervously, glancing behind the curtains to make sure no vampires or werewolves lurked there. She jumped when she heard a knock at the door.

"Kevin! I'm so glad—" Lucy cried as she threw open the double doors.

But it wasn't Kevin on the threshold.

Instead, Lucy found a little old lady in a maid's uniform clutching a bundle of fresh white towels.

"Let me help you with those," Lucy said, taking the towels from the woman's hands.

"Thank you," she replied, then the woman frowned. "You are so sweet, so innocent," she said as she violently shook her head.

"What's wrong?" Lucy asked.

"Nothing," the woman said.

"Something is definitely wrong," Lucy insisted.

The woman sighed and bit her lip. Lucy looked at her curiously.

"Please tell me," Lucy coaxed.

The woman nodded and whispered her warning. "I don't think you should stay in this room. Nobody stays in this room."

"Why not?"

"Because something terrible happened here."

"What do you mean?" cried Lucy, alarmed.

"This room is cursed," the old woman

continued. "I have heard the cries myself at night."

"The cries?" said Lucy. "What cries?"

"The cries of the ghost."

"Ghost?" said Lucy. "I don't believe in ghosts."

"But you should!" the woman insisted, gripping Lucy's arm. "This room is haunted by a spirit in torment!"

"Whose spirit?" Lucy asked, trying to humor the woman.

"The ghost of the woman who died here many years ago. The ghost of the murdered bride!"

Lucy blinked once. Then she calmly handed the clean towels back to the maid.

"We won't be needing these," she said.

Two minutes later, Lucy met Kevin in the hallway. He was alone, carrying two suitcases. She walked right up to him and said, "We're leaving."

"But—but—" Kevin stammered. "But we have a room!"

"A cursed room!" Lucy said. "A bridal suite of death! That's no place to spend eternity, let me tell you."

"What are you talking about?"

"There's a ghost. A ghost of a murdered bride. So we're leaving!" Lucy said, punctuating her words with a tug on his sleeve. A sharp tug.

"But we can't go," Kevin insisted. "We have no place to go."

"I don't care if we have to spend our wedding night at the airport," Lucy told him. "That's got to be better than this."

"But—"

"I'm telling you right now, Kevin Kinkirk, you can spend our wedding night with the ghost of a murdered bride, but I am out of here!"

# SIXTEEN

At nearly three o'clock in the morning, Kevin and Lucy dragged themselves back through the doors of the airport.

Though tired, both were grateful that the power hadn't yet failed here at the airport. Here the lights were bright. Not one ghost story or creepy hotel bellhop in view.

The return to normalcy gave Lucy hope. With luck, they could still get out of Glenoak and on to their honeymoon in the morning.

"I think the snack bar is open," Kevin said after they found seats. "Would you like something to eat or drink?"

At that moment the lights flickered. Then the terminal plunged into darkness.

"I guess not," said Lucy as she ran her fingers through her tangled hair. "Right now, I don't care about food. I don't even care about the lights. All I want is a warm bed—one that's not haunted," Lucy said with a tired sigh. "But I guess it's too late to go back to Glenoak now if we still want to try to fly out in the morning."

Kevin stifled a yawn. Then he plopped down in the seat next to hers. "I don't want anything, either. I just thought I'd ask."

Kevin held Lucy's hand. They sat together in silence, watching the rain fall and the lightning flash beyond the tall glass windows. The airport was quiet. There were no announcements because most of the flights had been canceled and the system was probably down anyway.

The few people inside the terminal were sprawled across chairs or spread out on the floor, trying to find sleep using coats, shirts, and even newspapers for a blanket.

Lucy gazed through the windows. She

felt miserable and lost and her mind was going around and around in a constant mental loop, like she was stuck in some kind of brain maze.

*Look at all the bad luck we've had,* she told herself.

With all the trials and tribulations, Lucy was really starting to wonder if marrying Kevin had been the right choice after all.

What if all their misfortunes were part of a very personal message from on high? A message that said, "You and Kevin should never have married because you are not meant to be."

Had Lucy done the wrong thing when she completely ignored all the signs and omens that the wedding shouldn't have taken place?

*Am I responsible for making a horrible mistake,* thought Lucy, *for ruining both Kevin's life and my own?*

"Kevin?" Lucy called softly. She felt him stir, and even in the darkness, she saw him open his eyes.

"What's wrong, Lucy?" he said sleepily.

"I need to talk to you."

Then, holding his hand in hers, Lucy told Kevin all the things she was thinking and all the emotions she was feeling.

She told him about her doubts before the wedding and now. She told him about her fear that their lives together would make them both unhappy.

Kevin listened patiently, without interruption. Then, when Lucy was finished, he wrapped her in his arms and held her close.

"Don't be silly, Mrs. Kinkirk," Kevin said. "We are meant for each other. I'm certain of that."

Lucy pulled away and stared at him.

"How can you be certain? How do you really, really know? You were in a relationship before. I'm sure you felt certain then. Absolutely sure that she was the right person for you—that you would spend your whole life together with her. Yet that relationship ended, right?"

"That was different," Kevin insisted.

"Different how?" Lucy said.

"She wasn't you."

"That's not an adequate reply," Lucy said, loud enough to elicit stares from some of the other people in the terminal.

"Sure it is," Kevin said.

Lucy shook her head. "With all that's happened today, how do you know that all the things that tried to halt the wedding— all the hassles we had and all the trouble our family members experienced getting to the ceremony—weren't part of some divine plan that was meant to stop the wedding before it happened?"

"First of all," said Kevin, "every wedding has problems. At least every wedding I've ever attended. Some people can't make it because of previous commitments, or some family members can't sit next to others because they don't get along. There's an argument, or the food isn't very good. . . ."

Kevin paused. Even in the dark he could sense that Lucy wasn't convinced.

"A wedding is like anything else in life, Luce—some of it goes smoothly, and some of it just falls apart. Nothing is perfect. And we have to make the best of our situation, no matter what that situation is. Make lemonade out of lemons."

"I'm not talking about lemonade!" Lucy cried. "I'm talking about us. About whether or not we were meant to be. I'm talking about bad omens and divine intervention."

Kevin laughed. "I think that if God didn't want us to marry, he could have stopped the ceremony anytime he wanted."

He touched Lucy's face.

"You're stubborn, Lucy . . . and willful. You're also smart and resourceful and beautiful and I love you very much, but if you wanted to get married and God didn't want you to . . . Well, I'd put my money on God and figure that the wedding was off."

"You're not even listening to what I'm saying," Lucy said angrily.

"Yes, I am," Kevin replied. "And you're just going through postwedding blues. The stress of the day's just got to you. I'm a cop. I'm used to stress."

"This is not stress!" Lucy insisted. "This is me honestly wondering if we were truly meant to be married. Here's how I feel: if all those bad omens were wrong, then prove it to me right now. Tell me one thing, one sign that we did the right thing when we both said 'I do.'"

"Well," Kevin said. "If you're looking for a sign, think about this: we first met in an airport, remember? And here we are spending our first wedded night to-gether . . . in an airport."

"But—"

"That's a sign, all right," Kevin insisted. "A sign that this marriage is meant to be. And, honey, if that's not good enough, then here's another sign, one that's even more important in the great scheme of things."

Kevin pulled Lucy close. For a mo-ment, she resisted, determined to keep arguing, but resistance is futile in the face of true love. Lucy quickly found herself surrendering to the sweetness of her hus-band's kiss.

When their kiss ended, Kevin smiled at his bride, and she smiled back.

"Now if that doesn't tell you we were meant to be together, then I don't know what will."

"Okay," Lucy whispered. "I give up. You win."

"We both do," said Kevin. "Look, I never expected a perfect wedding, and I really don't care about where we spend our honeymoon, either. If we have to spend the rest of our lives in this airport,

I'll be happy as long as we're together. As long as I'm spending my life with you."

"You're right," whispered Lucy. "It's how I feel, too."

Then Lucy rested her tired head on her husband's broad shoulder and snuggled in close. Soon the sound of the rain beating on the windows lulled her into a deep, dreamless sleep.

And that's how Lucy and Kevin spent the rest of their wedding night—in each other's arms.

Lucy felt a hand touch her shoulder. She squinted against the bright morning sun that streamed through the terminal windows.

"Wake up, sleepyhead," a familiar voice said softly. But it wasn't Kevin's voice.

Lucy opened her eyes fully. She was still wrapped in Kevin's arms, and her sister Mary was standing over her.

"Mary!" Lucy cried, jumping up and giving her a hug.

"Hey," said Matt with a wave as he approached them.

"Matt!" Lucy said, throwing her arms

around her brother's neck. "What are you doing here?"

"We could ask you the same question," Mary said.

"Flights were canceled," Lucy explained. "And the power went out here in the terminal."

"Well, everything is up and running now," said Mary. "I'm on my way back to work, and Matt is flying back to New York."

"Wow!" said Kevin. "I'd better see if our flight is ready."

The news turned out to be bad. Though the airport was officially opened, hundreds of people were now trying to get to where they were trying to get to before the storm hit. Flights were backed up, and no seats were available for Kevin and Lucy on any flight to their destination.

"I guess we should head for home, then," said Lucy.

Then she gazed into Kevin's eyes. "Or we could spend the rest of the honeymoon right here."

Kevin embraced his wife. "Whatever you want."

"You're not going anywhere," Mary said. "Except on your honeymoon."

With that, she marched off to her airline's ticketing desk.

"Got to go," said Matt, hugging Lucy and Kevin. "Mary managed to get me onto a flight leaving in half an hour. I know you two will be so happy together. Remember, kids, it just gets better every day."

With a wave, Matt went through the security gate and was gone to catch his flight.

"It was great seeing Matt," Lucy told Kevin.

"Yeah," Kevin replied. "I'm glad I got to know him a little better."

"I'm back," said Mary, waving two tickets in her hand. "Your plane leaves in less than an hour."

"Wow!" said Kevin.

"How?" cried Lucy.

Mary grinned. "Stick with me, kids, I've got clout. Now grab your gear and get on over to gate twenty-four. They'll be boarding you in a few minutes!"

# SEVENTEEN

Lucy checked the photographer's envelope. She'd thought it was empty, but there was one last picture. It was a photo Lucy hadn't even realized Mr. Fuller had taken. He'd snapped it back at the restaurant after the power had gone out. It showed Kevin and Lucy kissing in the warm, golden glow of a single candle.

Lucy smiled as she slipped the final picture into its plastic sleeve. Then she closed the wedding album and gently ran her fingers over the beautifully embroidered silk cover.

"All in all, it was far from the perfect wedding day," she admitted to her family.

"But it was my perfect wedding day, so even if I could, I wouldn't change a thing."

"Nothing?" asked Reverend Camden. "Not one little thing?"

Lucy shook her head.

"Even though lots of things went wrong, a lot of things went right, too, especially the two most important things: my family was there with me, and Kevin and I made it through the best and worst together. There's nothing more important than that."

"I think you've discovered the secret to a perfect wedding," Reverend Camden said. "It's simple, really. It comes down to one little word—"

"Love," said Mrs. Camden, smiling at her husband.

"Maybe weddings aren't so bad after all," said Ruthie after some thought. "I might even reconsider my plan to elope, if the circumstances are right."

"Those circumstances better include graduating high school and college first," Reverend Camden said.

"Hey," said Simon, "if Ruthie can live with the name Petrowski—not to mention spell it—then every other problem she encounters in life should seem pretty simple."

"Not funny," Ruthie said. "How old were you when you got married, Mom?" Ruthie asked.

"That's enough for this particular line of conversation!" Mrs. Camden declared, rising.

Lucy glanced at her watch and stood, too.

"I'd better go," she said. "I have an early class tomorrow."

Mrs. Camden frowned. "Then you won't see Kevin tonight?"

Lucy shrugged. "Probably not. I'll be asleep when he gets home, and he'll be asleep when I go to school in the morning."

Mrs. Camden touched her daughter's arm. "Don't worry," she said. "Kevin knows how important it is to spend time with you, doing things that couples do. I'm sure he'll make time for both of you to be together real soon."

"I hope so, Mom," Lucy said. "But even if he can't do that right away, I'll stick it out—for better or for worse."

"That's the vow, all right," said Mrs. Camden.

With a final hug, Lucy thanked her mother and sister for the beautiful wedding album, then said good night.

As she walked up to the apartment, Lucy hugged the album to her breast. To her it was much more than a book filled with memories—some of them bad, most of them good, and all of them cherished. To Lucy this wedding album was concrete proof that no matter how many storms life tossed at them, she and Kevin would weather them—together.

With that realization, Lucy promised herself that she would hold these memories in her heart, even on nights like tonight, when she couldn't hold her husband in her arms.

Smiling, she entered the garage and climbed up to the finished apartment. Yawning, Lucy pushed opened the front door.

Then she gasped in surprise.

The interior of the apartment was strewn with red roses! There were almost as many flowers as there were that Valentine's Day when Kevin first asked Lucy to be his wife.

But even better than the flowers, in the middle of the room stood Kevin, dressed in his best suit and lighting a candle. He gave Lucy a crooked smile and blew out the match.

"Surprise!" he said.

She ran into his arms.

When their kiss was over, Lucy stepped back and put her hands on her hips.

"Just how did you pull this one off?" she asked.

"It wasn't easy," Kevin replied. "But it was important that I do it—that we do it. We've both been working hard lately, and we need some time together."

"I concur," said Lucy.

"I asked your mother to stall you with the excuse that I had to work late. Then an emergency came up and I really did have to work late. So I had to make lemonade from a dish of lemons."

Kevin stepped over to the dining room table, which held more candles, a vase brimming with roses, and a casserole pan with a silver lid.

"I originally planned to cook you a gourmet meal," Kevin said.

"Unfortunately, I ran out of time. So, Mrs. Kinkirk, I'm afraid the menu tonight will be quite limited. . . ."

Kevin lifted the lid. "Take-out buffalo chicken wings and french fries."

Lucy laughed. "It sounds delicious."

Kevin offered Lucy a chair. "Your table awaits, Mrs. Kinkirk."

"Why, thank you, Mr. Kinkirk."

Kevin filled Lucy's glass. They made a toast, then they started to eat. Throughout the meal, they talked and laughed and talked some more. Finally, when the dinner was over, they snuggled up together on the couch.

"So," said Kevin. "Shall we look at those pictures?"

Lucy leaned against Kevin and kissed him.

"Later," she said. "But first, let's create some brand-new memories. . . ."